SAINT GRIT

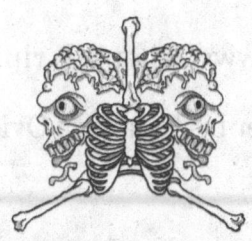

KAYLI SCHOLZ

Ghoulish Books
San Antonio, Texas

Saint Grit
Copyright © 2023 Kayli Scholz

ISBN: 978-1-943720-90-3

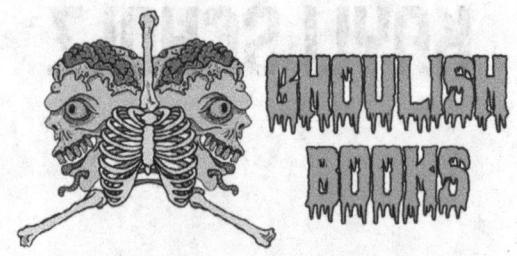

www.Ghoulish.rip

Cover by Alejandra Oviedo

This is for my late mother. I did it.

CHAPTER 1.

WE SMOKED GRASS with serene ritual on the hood of a Dodge watching blissed-out girls in halter tops rattling tambourines by the bonfire. Sugar Bends was a busted-down mill town but in July 1977, lovebug season, the girls came alive. The boys, dressed in Wranglers and drunk on Grit beer, milled around with affected swagger. That summer, everybody was pagan. Everybody at the bonfire had a spiritualist cousin who read tarot and studied astrology. Everybody was an expert on the mystic ladder.

Roger, in his macho delusions, called these nights *snapshots of occult matter*. We'd been going steady since May. He passed me the joint and I took a long hit, reveling in the euphoric headrush. The warm smell rose through the air lingering in a thick gray cloud.

"Nadine," Roger said. He leaned into me, sucking my tongue into his mouth. "I'm not going to wait any longer. I want you."

"I want you too."

I was rotten inside but not because I made Roger wait to screw me. I was rotten because of the witch growing inside of me, getting stronger every day. I was unmistakably beautiful; wavy steel blond hair, blue eyeshadow, black-winged eyeliner, and ruby-red lip gloss. I wore dramatic bell sleeves and midriff tunics. While the bonfire girls pinged for love on summer nights, I'd ritualized masturbation in the woods behind my house, so that way when Roger and I finally did have sex, it would be satisfying, empowering, and orgasmic like Donna's issues of *Ms.* magazine said. Sex magik.

I didn't believe in a lot of things. I believed I wanted to feel good all the time.

I unlinked my arm from Donna who'd been arguing with her boyfriend Ted all night. Our faces were flushed from the heat. Our hair smelled like Vidal Sassoon and cannabis. I passed Donna the joint, watching a black-bodied lovebug carcass writhe on the knee of my sparkling tights. I didn't bother flicking the insects away because they'd return copulating mid flight.

"Rural paganism," Roger said. He looked like every other guy in our class, long hair, mustache, and striped velour shirts.

"What about it?" I asked.

"See those gurus over there? They're closer to being pagans than this fake counterculture sideshow disguised in bonfire ash. Half of these girls couldn't differentiate Aleister Crowley from Jim Jones in a line-up. They treat Ed Warren like a *Teen Beat* pinup."

I clicked open a can of Grit beer unsurprised that Roger hadn't acknowledged Lorraine Warren. Roger was like that.

"Don't you know anything? Ghost hunters work with the church. Black magic is witchcraft," I said. "Superstition isn't new."

Roger glanced sharply at me, his eyes turning a shade darker. "I know what I'm talking about."

We watched the gurus. They came by all the time in their floor-length robes, offering peace and love in exchange for a dollar dropped into their burlap sacks. They didn't live in Sugar Bends. I don't think they lived anywhere. They were transients, free-spirits, probably filthy rich. They convinced everybody that everybody was worth loving, even if they weren't.

I knew everybody wasn't worth loving.

SAINT GRIT

My brother, Hatch, wasn't worth loving. He was the star quarterback, floating around the bonfire in a varsity jacket carrying around a steel guitar he'd snatched from a drunk girl. He dissolved into laughter. Everybody wanted to touch Hatch. Everybody wanted to tell him something. Everybody wanted to be in Hatch's rite of passage comprised of football, grabbing girls, and drinking. Hatch wasn't worth loving. The gurus didn't know that, no matter how many nights they came to the bonfires and smiled and waved.

Somebody pumped Talking Heads from a shag-carpeted van on the corner of Lake Odessa under a row of sparse pine trees. Donna went chasing after Ted. They'd been fighting all night. My high would wear off soon. The grass was weak. I wanted to leave. I wanted to have sex with Roger, finally.

"Women are witches with or without black magic," Roger said. "Did you see the way Donna treated Ted just now? I'd have slapped her if she talked to me that way. I'm glad you're not like that." He took the last hit of the grass, not offering me any more. "Most girls never shut up."

You couldn't see the stars out here in Sugar Bends, not by the lake, not in most places. The air was dusty from residual smoke rising through the air out of the sugarcane mill halfway across town. The stalks were burnings. We'd smell it until winter.

Me and Roger hopped off the Dodge and went into the woods surrounding the lake. A lot of kids were swimming drunkenly, flying off a rope tied to a hemlock. We walked among cottonwood leaves and stinky palmettos with red-stemmed brambles. The katydids rattled. The congregations of our peers quieted the further we hiked, crab grass and red buckeye grazing our calves.

I tore red buckeye off its stem, the dried thorn too. I was thinking how naïve women, centuries ago, would boil this buckeye with cat feces for unloving boyfriends and husbands and bray at the moon in unhinged anger to get loved better. Some things never change.

We arrived at an abandoned, pitch black hunting shed. It was the kind used for the boy scouts in the 1960s. There were termite holes all over the log-ceilinged frame, initials carved into the wood. *L+L, 1974, S+J, M+F.* Somebody had heaved a mattress onto the floor. It was caked in black mold and maggots wriggled out of a thick layer of rotting fruit, only half-digested in a dead crow.

This was it. I'd finally have sex.

I felt a jungle heat loom inside of me, ravenous. The backs of my knees were sweaty. We removed our own clothing. Roger pulled me onto the filthy mattress, his hands roving across my tits and thighs. We didn't kiss. When his hand drifted between my legs, a look of disgust came across his face as he snatched his arm away. I was embarrassed by how wet I was. I apologized.

"The girls I've been with don't get like that, Nadine," Roger said. He wiped his fingers off. "You better be clean. No VD or none of that."

"Of course, I'm clean. Don't get mad at me."

I was furious but wanted to hurry up, feeling flushed head to toe, nauseous from the trapped heat in the shed. I wanted to enjoy sex. I wanted to know what it felt like. I wanted to know what I'd conjured in the woods with my own lust that I was generous enough to give to Roger.

"You have—*you know*—a condom?" I asked.

Roger hovered over my body, guiding my hand to stroke his pink-fleshed dick. It was softer than I'd imagined. "Let me feel good, Nadine. Come on." He pushed into me without kissing me or looking at my body, and it was over in two minutes. He rolled off, panting.

Roger furrowed his brow. He was angry. He inspected the mattress while I was still on it, naked and sticky. He pulled my thighs apart.

"What's your problem?" I pushed away, grabbing my clothes and dressing as fast as I could.

"You lied to me is what, Nadine. You told me you were a virgin."

"I am! I was until a minute ago."

Roger ran his hands through his unwashed, smoky hair, throwing on the striped velour shirt.

"Say something!" I said.

He shoved his feet into some weathered sneakers. "You didn't bleed. I thought you were different. The girls I'm with bleed the first time."

"The girls you're with screw half the football team!"

"You're lucky I don't slap you."

"Roger," I said. "Wait. I'm sorry!"

We stumbled out of the shed. My body was still wet and unsatisfied. I'd practiced for a lightning orgasm from Roger for weeks. Suddenly, I was annoyed with Donna too, who eagerly told me about how great Ted was in bed.

I chased Roger back to the bonfire. We stood with the gurus who had returned at the midnight hour, the hems of their powder pink robes dragging in the dirt. Summer heat. I put my arm around Roger so he would forgive me, but it wasn't until a half hour later, while gazing in the Dodge's side-view mirror, trying to light a Salem, that I saw flecks of black eyeliner on the flesh around my eyes.

I forgot about the cigarette. I gripped the side-view mirror. My winged eyeliner. Roger's hair had invaded my face during his jack-hammer thrusts when he was on top of me, yelling at me in the shed, and now look. My eyeliner had smeared. I felt my gut catch fire with rage.

Donna drove me home. The windshield wipers did little to remove the caked-on lovebugs off the window. She was high as a kite, a little drunk. I didn't mention Roger.

The house was on Suwanee Road. There was a newly-installed post in the grass by the mailbox that read *Hatch Landing*, named after my brother, of course. It was a two-level house, big for Sugar Bends' standards, white wood frame like real country, a brick fireplace. We lived near Barrett's Cemetery on a lonely road. The house was surrounded in Spanish-mossed canopied southern oaks. The woods, a half-mile deep, didn't belong to our property line, fenced in by cheap metal fencing. It was where I did all my thinking, all of my private rituals, where I burned through anger.

The house was dead silent. Davey, my younger brother, slept in the room next to mine. Mom and Dad were across, and Hatch's room at the other end of the hallway. I peeled off the cowl neck tank top, changing into a red and black kimono. Once downstairs again, I gently closed the screen door on the back porch so it didn't snap and wake up the house.

I was alone and angry, traipsing up the wooded path to my spot, the trees casting shapes like shadows of tiny hands. The brambles were thick in my path. The air smelled musky this time of night when our poisonous tree branches got a little lift from a gust. It was a manchineel tree and Mom, in her patchwork kitchen apron, used to watch us from the porch to make sure we didn't get too close. Its shadow line was our cautionary mark and we never passed it as children.

The manchineel's sap was milky white and if touched caused boils or burns. If ingested, intestinal damage. When it rains—and it rains all the time this side of Florida—the poisonous sap becomes airborne. Mom worried about cancer. The manchineel was the furthest point from the house in our woods, *the* woods, and the yellow-green fruit that appeared seemingly overnight in winter was eaten by reptiles. We'd find them the next morning dead, belly-up, the fruit half eaten on the ground.

I drew a triangle in the dirt that was hard to see from the crab grass and weeds, the triangle that Roger believed he'd taught me to do, but I'd awoken once from a heavy dream where a woman in rags, with tree vine growing out of her head, poured oozing brimstone into my mouth.

Roger had nothing to do with my rituals. I was infuriated that Roger had almost made me cry. Nobody could do that. Almost. Almost made me cry. My mascara would've run too if I'd started crying. Roger hadn't given me an orgasm. He didn't even look at me. He didn't look at my body at all.

I uncurled the edge of the kimono, getting on my knees and then on my stomach in the triangle. I didn't need Roger to get off. I didn't need to hide under the covers in the dark after everyone was asleep to get off. I caressed myself until my clitoris pulsed for me to rub it. With my back to the sky and trees, the manchineel's branches shook in joyous disturbance. The ritual. I rubbed myself harder and when I finally came, without Roger, without Roger ruining my perfect eyeliner, I left the triangle. My face was hot.

I tied the kimono. With bare hands, sticky from orgasm, I grabbed a bramble from the manchineel and pulled it off the bark. The sap dripped onto the same hand. It didn't burn. It felt like the softest silk, festering like acid into my skin. I reentered the triangle, my clitoris still swollen in satisfaction, and instantly all three corners of my triangle caught flame. I didn't need ignition to start a flame, to finish my evocation, to hunt.

Grit beer. I remembered what I was going to call it. I needed a familiar, I needed the manchineel. I needed lust to empower me.

"I conjure thee to enter among me. I conjure thee to radical self-responsibility. I conjure thee to leave the celestials above my descendants. I conjure thee to enter among my five senses. I conjure thee Saint Grit into me."

The three flames grew high above my head like tiki torches and then evaporated just as fast. I left the triangle. My arms and legs tingled with wet heat.

I returned to the house and gulped four glasses of water. I went to bed. A man almost made me cry today. Never again. When I closed my eyes and was almost asleep, I heard a horn lament softly in my ear.

CHAPTER 2.

'D STARTED CALLING Mom and Dad by their real, non-maternal names the autumn I started junior year at Earl Jones High School. Only in private, naturally, because they wouldn't have tolerated their children calling them anything else. I'd gotten the urge to remove *Mom* and *Dad* from their identities after watching the ceiling fan, newly installed by George Boone—my father—go swirling off its gear and into the cherry-wood banister. I suspected my woodsy rituals had something to do with the energy that changed in our house after conjuring Saint Grit, causing the fan to snap off its axis and break.

It was November and Mom was Louise and Dad was George.

Louise and George Boone.

I got home from school one day to Louise milling around the kitchen over the sink, her dishwater hair pulled into a tight bun. She was always over the sink, cleaning something. She'd recently asked George to apply for a permit at city hall to have the manchineel torn down. She'd read in *Reader's Digest* that poisons, even moderately airborne, couldn't be cleaned with the palliative effects of elderberry syrup and granola. She wanted to eliminate cancer risks. George was too busy to consider it and thought Louise was overreacting. He was a shift manager at the lumberyard near Briggs Valley.

What was Louise's life outside of standing in front of the sink? What was her life after taking care of three brats, all of whom were ungrateful for Louise's domestic labor hanging linen and driving us to school? She was joyless. She suffered a chronic dry cough in the daytime from the sugarcane burnings. It was almost time for the harvest and it would be six months before Sugar Bends was under smoke again. No wonder Louise worried about cancers, I thought. Dumb to go out thinking you could cure cell mutation with berry sugar.

I didn't have the patience for Louise after she began collecting bicentennial music boxes when Jimmy Carter got elected. She had about half a dozen of the stupid music boxes on the brick mantel in the living room. Upon opening each bronze box, a fairy flute would play from faux grass with paper children flying kites made out of origami. Every afternoon, during the quietest part of the day, Louise would carefully open each box to hear the flute. It embarrassed me, her need to play with music boxes.

I decided to lend some drama to Louise and George's marriage by concocting a lie I drew out of thin air during one of Louise's sink-cleaning afternoons. She ate cracked peanuts out of a dish, looking tired.

"How's Roger's studies coming along?" Louise asked. *Studies*. She looked about fifteen years older than she was, gazing out the window at our old kid swing in the backyard.

"Roger is fine," I began. "Mom, I have something to tell you about Dad."

"Oh?"

"After school, me and Donna, we stopped by Sugar's Market. Donna needed some ibuprofen. Well," I sighed, putting on a timid voice, "Dad was there. You know that lady that works at the bank? Well, he was talking to her, *like*, really talking to her. Smooth-talking, if you know what I mean."

Louise poured Comet into the sink. "I'm afraid I don't."

Davey bounded through the front door and into the kitchen. He was fourteen but acted seven. Louise asked him why he was late. "Band practice," Davey said. "You never remember."

Davey grabbed the glass container of cottage cheese out of the fridge and scooped out a chunk with his index and middle finger, licking it. I grimaced. He left his school books on the kitchen table for somebody else to move and made a lot of noise going up the stairs.

"Dad was with another lady. The lady from the bank. He didn't know that I saw him."

Louise turned off the faucet. "What do you want me to say, Nadine? Your father is not just your father, he is also a man."

I'd wanted to see her reaction and got it. Louise's reaction was indifference. It fascinated me, how a woman standing in a kitchen that she'd probably never enjoyed a meal in because she was always scrubbing and boiling potatoes, didn't express any cause for concern about her husband talking intimately with another woman.

George Boone's dependable aggression was only surpassed by his reticence. He probably nodded his head half-approvingly when I was born, eager to get home and go to bed. If it wasn't structured for him, he didn't want it, and would dispose of it.

Days after the big homecoming game, we went out to dinner as a family. The station wagon trundled down the winding road to Placerville where the steakhouse was. I'd been experiencing a static hum in my ears, so low, I had to concentrate to hear it. Donna said I needed my ear canal drained. I'd get to miss a day of school, maybe two days, if I carried on about it. But telling Louise meant inviting her into the private black space between Saint Grit and I. The static noise stayed with me through the entire dinner. It was not a coincidence. I had conjured this.

The low static was the beginning.

We sat in a booth and Hatch looked so satisfied with himself in his letterman jacket, getting recognized by not just a waiter but several patrons, including George's work friends. George drank bourbon and Louise, embarrassed by her sip of champagne, merely nibbled on a salad. Hatch consumed two prime rib cuts, mashed potatoes, asparagus, and dinner rolls. George nudged Hatch to take a sip of bourbon, just one, we won't tell Mom. He stuffed his face and he didn't look at me through dinner. The boys ate steaks. Louise and I ate salads.

George almost bought the farm when Davey announced that he was trying out for water polo in January. George said he didn't know what the hell water polo was and he should know better than to try out for anything other than football.

George made us all take pictures with the good family polaroid on the football field upon driving home from the steakhouse. I'd come to find out later in the week my photo was blurred by a watery blue mark over my face. Louise said she'd need to take the camera into the shop. It must've been where I was standing, she said.

I knew better.

When everyone retreated to their bedrooms for the night, Hatch left to go out with his friends in the TransAm, gifted to him by our uncle last Christmas that he parked proudly on the street. Hatch didn't have a curfew. I wasn't allowed out after midnight unless I was babysitting.

I sneaked into Hatch's bedroom to snoop through his private things; drawers, letters, jeans, tin cans, and storage chests. In the tin can was my stolen cigarettes, which I promptly took back. I flipped through his stacks of *Penthouse*. Sections of the magazine implied violence with captions like "Brutal Gangbang, Rough Teen Sluts." My intention was to tear out the pages and show them to Donna, tell her that I found these in Ted's truck when he drove us all home the other day, but I let it go. I'd save that reaction for another time.

I returned to my vinyl-stickered bedroom, paisley and paper flowers, feeling a sharp pain in the back of my neck. I rubbed my neck and noticed the leaves etched under my fair skin around my elbow. It felt like the ground outside. I pulled at the edge of the growth until the leaf slid out, and then another leaf. My ankles hurt, too.

On the first spring full moon, 1978, the enormous gulf between me and Saint Grit became as small as a coin. I was unraveling. Starry-blue eyed marks on the polaroid and shaking ceiling fans were nothing but checked boxes in comparison to the noise that erupted from Mr. Jenkins' English class after homeroom.

Roger screamed. He was having a nightmare.

I'd never heard a noise so perpetually barbarian. We rose from our desks, murmuring among ourselves as Mr. Jenkins told everybody not to touch drooling, wet-lipped Roger.

"He's having a bad dream," Mr. Jenkins said. "Let's give him space."

I knew better. This was my doing. Roger was having a bad dream that I haunted. I was the thing he was running from in the dream, and he *wailed* for me to get away from him.

When the nurse arrived, I heard Mr. Jenkins ask if it was a drug-induced seizure. Two EMTs showed up with a transport bed. They picked up Roger by his mustard-stained armpits, tilting his head forward as he dry-heaved, opening his eyes in what I could only assume was mid-terror. He locked eyes with me, halfway across the classroom.

"You!" Roger said. "It was you, you fucking witch! You were there! It was her!"

Everybody turned to look at me. Everybody knew me as Roger's steady girlfriend.

I decided, for the sake of appearances, I was not there, wherever Roger said I was, and as Roger was frantically strapped to a bed and taken away by ambulance, I asked to speak to Principal Tate in the office. I pleaded for early dismissal. I needed to see my mother and have a ginger ale. I needed to know Roger was going to be okay and wasn't using drugs, *anything* but drugs, Principal Tate. Principal Tate wrote me a pass and I walked the sidewalks the long way home, whistling breezily to myself. I didn't care who heard me whistle.

Sugar Bends brooded strange weather and sordid people, the fetid smell of moss and wet sugarcane rich in the air. I was full of darkness like the town was. The women here carried themselves with exhaustive despair, like they were always walking somewhere wretched. The men, too, bewitched by natural things, standing under the hemlocks, unsure of how they got there or where they were going, except they were drawn to the trees to only turn around and go back to work.

It happened to George. I saw it happen. Once when I was a little girl, unaware of my darkness, I saw George amble out of our house on Suwanee Road and hurry down the sidewalk that turned the corner toward the cemetery. He looked up at the trees like he'd start howling like a wolf. He looked over his shoulder, caught me looking at him, and we never spoke about it.

I walked for a mile on the railroad tracks waiting for the familiar rumble from a supply train. I liked waiting until the last minute to tumble off the tracks, the dirt and rocks blowing back in my face as the train rolled by. But there were no trains this afternoon and my walk took me through the woods to Tidioute, where they'd erected a mobile home community that was taken care of by Roger's father, a foreman. The double-wide trailers had a coat of new white paint and tarps strapped to the tin roofs to keep the smoke out. I wondered if Roger's father was as bad at being a man as Roger pretended to be.

Roger liked to have me under his arm at the football games, at the bonfires, and at the diner when we had nothing else to do but sit in the booth and play with the jukebox. A trophy. He didn't need to hear me talk. Sex with Roger made me dwell on the shape of his skull and brain. The anatomy of vertebrae and neck appending his brain fascinated me. I could've been headless, decapitated by the train, my guts spilled all over the tracks, and Roger would still get off, pumping senselessly into my body. I was a receptacle.

I lit a cigarette, whistling between hits. I couldn't place where the sprightly tune came from but when I looked up into the slice of blue sky through the towering hemlocks, I felt my face caressed by what I only assumed was Saint Grit walking with me.

I crossed Harris Road near the River Cross where eighteen-wheelers rode by at odd hours. They picked up plastics and lumber. That's all Sugar Bends was: plastics, lumber, sugar, deadweight. But I had the trees, the manchineel. All of this delicious poison inside of me, boiling through my organs and arteries, fattening bubbles out of my veins like the leaves erecting beneath my skin.

On Harris Road a new shopping mall was going up by the funeral parlor. The shopping malls were all over Florida now, and Sugar Bends would attempt jonesing functionality like the rest of the skunk-stink sinkhole. Construction workers in yellow hard hats grabbed their toolbelts suggestively, lapping tongues, catcalling. Donna would get mad at these things. She'd find them threatening. They didn't know about the poisonous tree growing as an entity within me. I had power, too.

The sidewalks got busier after the elementary school let out. The crossing guard came out and I was no longer alone, crossing through Barrett's Cemetery toward home on Suwanee Road. I could see from the sidewalk that Louise and George were arguing in the knee-high grass that they were too lazy to mow and take care of. Our crooked mailbox had been uprooted out of the ground.

Next to the planter and tomato bed was a new

manchineel tree, blooming, luscious, full forest green. Full poison.

"Don't get near it, Nadine," George warned. He had a lick of sweat under his lip. Louise cried. He looked like he wanted to strike her, and maybe he already had. Her face was bright red, her apron bunched around her hips. "I told you to get these trees taken care of, Louise! Now look'it the problem! Growing like weeds!"

"It's beautiful," I said, smiling.

CHAPTER 3.

PROM NIGHT FOR the senior class meant George and Louise were proud of their son. They'd purchased a shiny new camera from Radio Shack. It was an expensive purchase. Hatch was going with a junior, Lindsay, a friend of mine and Donna's.

"Hey, Hatch, can you come and help me?"

I was alone in the kitchen, having overturned the coffee maker and toaster for appearances. I knocked over a chair so the noise echoed upstairs. Hatch, annoyed, reluctantly came to my rescue, right in the midst of throwing on his long necktie over his rented tuxedo. He'd made a big deal about wearing the necktie instead of a bow tie.

"Davey's snake went down the disposal. I saw it—*look*—I can still see it. Please. I don't want the snake to go down the pipes."

"Nadine, are you being serious right now?"

It couldn't have been a worse time for Hatch, hours before prom, before the pictures had been taken. Lindsay would show up any minute. This was ludicrous for him that I needed assistance. Unacceptable.

"Come on. Just pull the snake out, will you?"

Hatch sighed. He approached the sink like I'd asked him to move Mount Rushmore. He rolled the tux's sleeve up to his forearm, sticking his hand in.

"I don't feel anything," he said.

"It's real deep in there. I saw it," I said. "You know I'm afraid of snakes. Let me show you." I put on a show insisting I could get the orange-scaled corn snake myself and I didn't need Hatch's help. I pushed him out of the way and put my face against the disposal, agreeing the snake *was* in deeper than I thought but we could reach it if we just looked first. "You have to look, Hatch. Don't just grab."

"Maybe it's stuck in the pipes."

Hatch bent forward so his face was next to the drain, looking at the bolts and blades embedded in the plaster. I gasped, looking down at my feet. A pile of leaves from the manchineel surrounded me.

"What?" Hatch said. He was still face-down in the sink, trying to see Davey's snake.

"Nothing," I said, gathering the leaves one by one and stuffing them in the trash can. "Thought I saw the snake slither out."

Saint Grit's horn softly lamented in my ear, and the lights above the kitchen flickered once, twice. The disposal kicked on. Hatch's necktie twisted around the blades, choking him so his head was violently thrusted into the plaster. His skull clunked on the faucet. He screamed like Roger did back in that classroom, calling out my name to help him.

"Hatch!" I said, full of convincing fear.

Hatch gasped for air. He begged me. I'd never had anybody beg me to do anything before. His skin turned purple, his eyes a shade of red like the buckeye around Lake Odessa. The blades spun harder. I heard a cracking malfunctioning within the plaster, and Hatch was pulled down further so his nose was smashed, his chin raised slightly up the blades that had fully eaten the necktie. At some point, Hatch quit writhing. He collapsed. I dramatically fell to his side while George, Louise, and Davey rushed in from outside, shouting, "We couldn't get in! The front door was locked!"

Saint Grit had locked the door. I knew it.

At the hospital that evening, a nurse in triage brought us into a tiny powder blue room. I knew what the tiny room

was for. Somebody in black robes with a pale face and cold hands would ask if they could pray for us. I felt *rabid* over this. I wanted to touch myself, to get off, not to the new death, but to the power I conjured and contained within me, as primitive as if I'd came at Hatch with a bow and arrow. A true conjuring.

Louise sobbed uncontrollably. Sobbing like Roger, like Hatch, like myself the night that Roger had screwed me and fucked up my black winged eyeliner that I had a gift for penciling just right. I'd never seen George look like that either—unmoored. I didn't recognize him. What would he miss most? The congratulatory handshakes from poverty-lined townies at the market, or the football games where George could jerk-off to high school boys playing football? I watched George, the three of us sitting in the hardback chairs, surrounded by pamphlets and prayer books, his eyes swelling with tears.

I made George cry.

I had to fake cry. I had to. Davey wasn't crying, not yet, but he was clearly bothered. He looked like he might vomit, his eyes closed like a fist so he didn't have to see George and Louise crying.

From in the powder blue room, there were medicinal smells of adhesives and rubbing alcohol. Heavy trays were being zipped down hallways. A doctor came in, not a triage nurse, closing the door. Louise collapsed to the floor. I'd never seen anything like it in my life. She just flung herself. It looked out-of-body. Pathetic. Her knees on this filthy floor where hundreds of others had wept for their cretinous loved ones begging for one more chance. I couldn't laugh. I had to stifle it. I grabbed onto Davey's jacket, and he grabbed onto me, and I watched George fall upon Louise and scream synchronously in agony.

As the doctor offered condolences for our loss, George was handed a telephone from the triage nurse to call the funeral parlor. Done and done. I quietly left the room as Louise's weeping became more tortured, heading into a restroom. My jaw hurt from stifling my smile. Hatch was dead. My brother was dead. Wait until the kids at prom heard. I made him cry. I grabbed some stiff paper towels from the dispenser and rubbed them all over my face so it looked like I'd been crying. I rubbed my face raw and forced myself into hyperventilation by breathing rapidly through one nostril like I saw in health class. When I was satisfied with how bloodshot my eyes looked, I went back to the powder blue room. I cried that this freak accident was all my fault and I joined Louise on the floor in performative grief.

CHAPTER 4.

THE SUGARCANE BURNINGS started early that year in the spring of 1978 on the cusp of Gemini season. Black rain season. I'd pull on a kimono and tiptoe out into the early morning light under the manchineels, hold the water hose up to the sky and place my thumb over the spout to watch the poisonous vapors spray our land. On the same weekend of the first black rain, George packed up Hatch's TransAm. He didn't tell us where he was going or when he'd be back, or if he would be back. Two men gone, Hatch and George, in the span of three months.

It was better this way.

Louise grieved. For a couple of weeks, a priest came that the neighbor sent over. And then the neighbors quit coming with rafts of food and clusters of peonies and handwritten condolences they labored over like it fucking mattered. The good food was gone and Louise was cooking her slop for me and Davey again.

My ritualized spells turned into blueprints for the darkness incubating inside of me in the tail of Saint Grit. By the time Gemini season was over, I'd taken leaves from the manchineel and stuffed them into year-old pinecones that were still strewn around the yard in damp piles. The delicate wooded squares were folded in from moldy, white fungi, but I stuffed the squares, lighting fire to them when the black rain was at its thickest part of the day after sundown. The manchineels were cold to the touch, and the one that had bloomed overnight last winter when I'd walked home after Roger was wheeled away by ambulance, still thrived over the black soiled planter.

We had to get jobs that summer. Louise drove me around town. She made a whole to-do about Davey training for water polo at the community center and how he wouldn't have time for work. Davey got to miss a lot; the cleaning out of Hatch's things that Louise, not George, packed into the attic, the job hunting, cleaning the drafty, dusty house, cooking.

"Is that fair, Mother?" I asked.

Louise took up smoking Pall Malls that spring, but only while driving. With her arm out the window, her worried eyes looking properly 1978 like this was her life and it was almost over.

"Is what fair, Nadine?"

"Davey doesn't have to work because he's playing water polo boy."

"If he makes it to the regional, he'll make state—that's what the coach says. He could go *pro*fessional by the time he's eighteen," Louise said. "He'll make more money than we ever could ringing up yams at a cash register or separating plastic utensils at the factory. You're going to learn, young lady, that life isn't fair. Just look at what happened to Hatch."

Louise and I both applied for the same jobs on Placerville Road; Sugar's Market, Hunky Dory's diner, the drugstore, the florist. We'd work in plastics if we were lucky.

I spent the days at my new job at the market dwelling on how Hatch died. His guttural *howl* for help. At night, after my shift, I lie awake with the window perched open, the hot air wrapping around the bed sheet, hoping the black smoke would penetrate our vents and down into Louise's pink lungs, tarring them black.

As hot summer came to pass, George's postcards, stamped from Mojave County somewhere deep in the Arizona mesas, became fewer. He never wrote *I Love You* on postcards. They said *Behave*. They said *God Bless*. "This is what men do," I told Louise, whose hands shook searching the postcard for a telephone number or a sign of affection. But he'd written nothing of sentimentality.

Louise lost some of her wife-stricken grief when she got a job at a florist shop on Placerville Road near the market. She worked four afternoons a week. When she wasn't busy arranging spray-painted roses, she was stuck on cell mutation and all the horrible things that could grow inside of your body and you wouldn't know it until it metastasized your skeleton. "The black rain," she cried. "It's going to make us sick." She coughed throughout the night, barely making it to the kitchen for water without falling to her knees.

Roger, too, suffered. I showed up to the bonfires every hot night where Roger, not so long ago, danced to Fleetwood Mac in the smoke and embers, drunk, joining the chorus of derisive laughter from our peers. He'd been free and popular.

"What's the matter, Roger?" I asked.

When he saw me approaching him from the brambles, he stumbled over skunkvine and yelped, running into the woods. I followed him, the red brambles scratching at my legs, the only light leaking from the lighthouse above the hill, only to find Roger squatting behind a live oak, thinking I couldn't see him. He looked like he was running from a wolf, or a bear, hiding for his dear life.

"Roger? Where are you?" I played. "I miss you."

"Leave me alone!" He hitched his breath, grabbing onto the cottonwood leaves as the tree bark crumbled. "Leave me *alone!*"

His voice trembled.

That same summer, I visited Roger in his dreams, his nightmares, in the trailer park. Saint Grit guided me. I felt orbited, as if my back was flat against the ceiling above where Roger and his father watched a baseball game on the T.V., drunk on Grit beer. I could feel Saint Grit moving inside of me like a growing infant, rolling, stretching, making noise. The low-rise static that had pulsed through my eardrums and in our house on Suwanee Road was louder than bombs, and soon enough, the people around me could hear it too, including Louise, including Roger.

My physical self was in bed in my room, the trees rustling, the static-hum rising. But I could see the trailer. It was like looking through a foggy-lense binocular. Roger could feel me and sense me, and he spilled his can of beer as the smell of Saint Grit, myself, rank with wet earth and the wood, came upon him.

"Please stop," he muttered.

"Look at me, Roger."

Roger's dad sniffed the air, flat on his back with his legs stretched onto the arm of the couch. "What's that stink?"

"Roger, look at me," I said.

"*Please, please, please* stop."

His dad barked, "Boy, what in the hell are you stuttering like that for?"

"Nadine, please—" Roger rolled over onto his side. "I know it's you. Please leave me alone. I'm sorry."

Near Labor Day, when the house was filled up with the smell of cigarette smoke and meat stewing in the crockpot, Davey and I had work to do. We ribboned yellow tape across the healthy tomato bed and hydrangea planters adjacent to the manchineels to the side of the house. The skinny ones with twisted branches that I could see from my bedroom window. Louise raised hell at city hall. She wanted the trees chopped down, pronto. She told ordinance she could smell the poison and it was giving her sores on her knuckles and on the bridge of her nose and lips. But Louise couldn't afford to file for the permit to have the manchineels removed, and Briggs Valley had a little army of environmental flag wavers ready to strike if somebody ripped up the natural land.

"Dad said grassroots lobbyists are hippies," Davey said. He was fifteen now and talked about George all the time. He snapped the bright yellow tape off with his teeth, slapping the edges onto the rim of an empty flower pot. (Louise had replanted the blue hydrangeas by the porch, afraid it would rain and the poisons would seep into the soil.)

"George is about a year away from being six feet underground."

"Why do you say that? Hey, Nadine, I said, why the hell do you say that?"

When Davey was angry with me, his lip quivered. He always looked on the verge of tears like his pouting mother. I smiled gently at him. "I'm preparing you," I said.

I didn't bother dodging out of the way of the treeline when the wind picked up and the branches shook, and it started raining. Davey watched me, safely from the porch, surrounded by petunias, the broken step, and his beat-up baseball glove.

The rain fell as the sky struck a shade of blue gold. A black figure floated from the open window on the floor above, catching Davey's eye. There was an uninterpretable static, a voice, maybe the horn, that carried down to the porch. "Something's wrong with you," he said. "You're dark and mean."

On Labor Day it was the night before school started. Louise caught me in the triangle in the woods under the manchineels. I felt the evening air against my skin under the kimono, stroking between my legs. I knew she was there, leaning into the shadows, her wretchedness watching me as I looked up at the visible cone of light that cut from the second story to the wooded outskirts. Down on my knees, I looked over my shoulder and smiled wickedly at her. I didn't bother to quit touching myself. I rubbed harder. A high wind rose and Louise brought her hand to her appalled expression, stepping backward. She turned as if struck in the face and ran back into the house framed in low shadow light.

As I came, sap dripped onto my back and I felt bony, wet fingers glide over my jawbone and up the back of my skull.

In the full-dark, I walked down Mowry Road to the slaughterhouse past the old dairy farm under the water tower. The sky was solid indigo. I shone a slim flashlight to guide my path to the industrial part of town that was cloaked in darkness with hot barns and torso-high weeds. The railroad would be noisy this time of night, but not yet, and although the screeching trains could be heard all the way out here, they rumbled by over a mile away. There was mud and rock and weeds, deep in The Bends where the putrid whiff of manure and blood and urine climbed over the fence. Nobody would catch me out here in the pasture and the ambling Doberman left me alone because I was a witch, and whatever the Doberman smelled on me, he didn't like. He retreated, whimpered, and sniffed the air. There was something inside of me that wasn't to be messed with, not even by a feral dog.

The slaughterhouse was still operable in this broken mill town, hauling pig anus and pig belly onto the night trains, visible from the water tower adjacent to bunched treetops spilling shadows onto the pasture. There were turned over barrels and rotted machinery grinders, their metal parts speckled broken and black, looking ancient in the daytime.

The edges of my kimono got caught on the pointy timber as I jumped the weathered fence, crawling through an open window into the slaughterhouse. Dead pigs hung on metal slabs; their snouts turned toward the ground. The rancid stink washed over me. The trapped heat made the whiff of pig blood and manure rotten. I located the serrated blades and cylindrical saws hanging on the walls next to the slaughtered pigs. Mostly clean instruments.

I waved the flashlight around the room, pausing at the bone saws. I grabbed a serrated bone saw and hitched the door beyond the dead pigs, stepping into pitch-black unremitting heat. It was insufferably humid. With the bone saw gripped in my right hand like a pipe, I sidestepped straw and horse manure that caked my ankles. The squishing wet sensation was not as harsh as the smell.

The swine oinked and grunted in the tight pen, waiting in their filth to die. One of the pigs raised its snout and made wet noises at me. It sounded like Roger suffering a night terror; same species, same helpless sounds. I felt my way through the darkness because the beam from the flashlight wasn't enough, the whites of the swine's eyes coming into vision. In the corner of a bale of hay, I stood in manure and grabbed a handful of gray-tufted fur between its floppy ears. The pig whinnied.

I jammed the bone saw sideways into its fat neck, forcing the serrated blade into the tight muscle. Pools of blood spurred, like a blast at first, and then like lava. I could see the blood bubble in the darkness, and I removed the bone saw and then forced it back inside the neck, going further, twisting and gutting, up to my forearm in cartilage. I yanked the tufted fur vertically and it peeled off its skin. The other swine in the adjacent pens grunted.

I didn't have trouble gutting the pig. My body strength, hulking and tenacious. I went from the other side of its neck with the bone saw, jamming and twisting. I went down into its breast bone, using my right foot to finish off its lung capacity as the mammal bled out. Its pink ears flopped to one side and its eyes looked forced open. Its brain leaked out the mouth, and when I couldn't muster the strength to saw anymore, I grabbed an axe and chopped the rest of its head off, finishing the job. I left the rest of its body and bones in the hay and bagged the swine's head in a black bag I found in a supply closet.

I heaved the pig's head all the way home.

Ravens and magpies would have licked up any trace of blood I dripped onto the dirt road. I didn't see it, I didn't care.

The next morning, Louise knocked on my bedroom door while I was getting ready for school, sitting at the heart-shaped vanity. Senior year. Roger wouldn't show up. He was too haunted.

"Hello, Louise," I said, applying black eyeliner.

Louise looked inconsolable. I thought perhaps Davey had fallen and died in front of the kitchen sink, too.

"Nadine," she began. Her crow's feet swelled with tears. I noticed in the mirror's reflection, the blood stains in the crick of her fingernail beds. "I never want to see that again. Please. May God have mercy on us."

I'd planted the pig's head in bed with her where George used to sleep.

"Don't ever follow me into the woods again," I said. "Unless you want to clean up the loins. There's plenty more swine in this town."

Louise quietly shut my bedroom door, went down the hall to wake Davey for school, and made coffee. She'd had to clean it up. I noticed a drip of the pig's blood dripping from her pink floral nightgown.

CHAPTER 5.

THE FIRST TIME that Saint Grit left her symbol in Sugar Bends was in the fall of 1984, etched into the water tower. Her *mark* looked like it had been a fast job, like scratch marks, two jagged lines crossing over an oval. Her mark reminded me of the budding, stone-hard horns between a baby goat's soft ears. Even the house on Suwanee Road was marked by Saint Grit; deep, black scratches on the wooden panels like somebody trying to escape from the outside to get in.

I took great satisfaction in my primitive power these days. The sound of the primordial horn in the distance, feminine and wild. I peeled manchineel leaves out of the heel of my foot and from beneath my fingernail beds. My hair didn't need to be washed anymore. And food and drink for nourishment and nutrition didn't sustain me. I was replenished with electrolytes and nutrition from the sap and pruned leaves, by my own orgasm. My bones were healthy. I required less sleep; sometimes none at all. I was strong. My skin was beautiful, free of blemishes. My body was always satisfied.

Saint Grit was a separate skeleton inside of me.

Halloween was around the corner as an unusual cold front arrived in the form of fog. Jack-o-lanterns were aglow in windows and stuffed scarecrows on porches. I left pumpkins on the porch to rot. Louise hated deformity. I liked the pumpkins that way, slacking grin and choppy eyes, as pumpkin guts poured out helplessly in the sun, covered in ants. Deformed.

SAINT GRIT

The turning point for Sugar Bends in 1984 was the new plastics mill down by the water tower and dairy farm in Briggs Valley. Plastics supplied our wasteland with its economy. Everybody had a job, for now. Townies were bothered by Saint Grit's symbols, first looking as commonplace as graffiti. *What are they?* The endless musings occurred in the factory break rooms and in the check-out lines. Some people didn't care at all. But after the water tower, Saint Grit marked live oak trees and sidewalks, lumber piles at the lumber yard, and the baseball field. They were as if a *warning* was in place.

I was twenty-four that October, and worked in a nondescript office at the mill facing the green and yellow sugarcane stalks.

Before the harvest, the dense black smoke looked like a catastrophe billowing up from ground war. During my smoke breaks, I watched the tired men on harvesters. Some of them, I regularly screwed, some dated, but nothing serious. I shared the ancient filing system and mail room with Cassidy Burke—*the office girls*, they called us—we also shared a desk and a rotary phone. There weren't computers at the mill. The filing system hadn't been updated since 1976, creaky, alphabetized rows. There was a calendar on the wall of a half-naked woman with creamy breasts looming over us that the day shift manager tacked to the wall and changed diligently on the first of every month.

"The men get crazy eyes for you here," Cassidy once said. She always chain-smoked at the desk, a pack a day, like me. She looked like Debbie Harry. "What's your secret?"

"Ritual," I said.

Cassidy was not yet afraid of me.

She didn't know what I was capable of nor that the coven we attended together out in Briggs Valley was not for shits and giggles, or self-love spiritual sisterhood, but where I scouted for other women who carried my darkness.

Cassidy didn't know that I would hang her upside down between two hemlocks so her joints snapped out of their sockets, her limbs stretched apart with goat's horns sticking out of her mouth and rectum.

"Ritual," Cassidy said. "Sounds exciting."

We watched the mill men carry on in the field. Something happened and we'd find out within the hour that the green and yellow stalks were turned over, uprooted, and twisted in bunches. Tied. The fronds were tied up with sticks in the same jagged, oval symbols that Saint Grit marked the water tower with. There were tree branches, too, the spike of the timber sticking out like a saw. The mill was frantic.

The men, in their work coveralls and utility belts, were too caught up in the analytics of whose watch this happened on. They'd have to suffer for somebody else's actions.

"Sticks," I said, looking at Cassidy. "What do you think that means?"

"They look like witch totems."

I glanced sharply at her. "What do you know about witch totems?"

"Didn't you ever play that game as a kid—*Find the Witch*? You made a totem out of construction paper and somebody had to hunt you and the paper-totem." She laughed, shaking her head at the frantic scene on the field. "They're carrying on about grass."

The mill men threw their arms up, even a hardhat went flying. I caught the sight of a single flame in the grass. The emergency sirens rang inside the factory, the ones that went off only in a real emergency, like an injury or a tornado watch.

"Witch totems and games," I said. "Sounds like you've spent too much time with our coven girls."

"The hell I do," Cassidy said. "Hey, you got yourself a night on the town with that fellow from the textile factory hanging out with the coven girls."

"Who do you think's doing it?"

"Ritual," Cassidy teased. "Oh, lighten up. Probably that high school gang. One of them, the oldest boy, he's got a motorcycle now." Cassidy was not unlike Donna, convinced the markings were a sign of infuriating teenage vandalism.

I watched the men fussing, the black smoke drifting skyward off the fronds. The manager phoned the office, asking Cassidy to grab the polaroid in the drawer and document the "heathen activity" before one of the guys in the field crushed it with his gorilla boots. We grabbed hard hats and stepped onto the smoky field walking through the rows of sugarcane; the tops charred from this morning's sweeping burn.

"Don't get too close to it," Cassidy said, peering through the bulky lens of the camera. "Move—you're in my shot."

"It is a totem," I said.

It was a witch's totem. Saint Grit's totem. It was meant for me like an offering, although nobody else knew that. A flame rose out of small bones and bunched manchineel leaves that didn't burn, with a jagged hemlock branch tied up in sticks to a black horn once belonging to a small animal. Stickied grass and sap were caked onto the curved part of the animal's horn. A euphoric cold wave coursed through my body, followed by a sheen of sweat on my face. I knelt to the flame and inhaled, instantly satisfied. I resisted the urge to touch the flame, lifting the totem and cradling it against my sweater where I caressed the small bone.

"Wash your hands," the manager said. "Those vandals take dumps on public property all the time!"

"Nadine—" Cassidy said. "Maybe you shouldn't touch that."

That evening, after work, I brought the totem home with me so the mill men wouldn't crush the branches or smash the horn with an ax. It was mine, after all. I parked the Pinto by the mailbox and wicker sign.

Welcome to Hatch Landing.

Hatch was buried at Barrett's Cemetery which I frequented, whistling while I walked, kicking soil on his grave if nobody was looking. Davey, on the other hand, hadn't left a mark in Sugar Bends unlike his dead brother. Davey left home at seventeen to play water polo in Pensacola as Louise's health deteriorated. He didn't call much, not unlike George. On occasion when Davey phoned, the static of Saint Grit was so loud between us, hitch-pitched and tinny, the calls eventually dropped altogether. It frightened Davey, the noise.

Louise lived upstairs in Hatch's old bedroom, sick with advanced emphysema that left her on an oxygen tank in the days subsequent to the burnings. The bedding had been changed, but not washed. The room had a slick smell of dampness. Her deterioration left her feeble and depressed. We could not afford a pulmonologist and her inhaler had expired. Louise awoke in the middle-of-the-nights to brutal coughing fits. I'd listen to her drag herself into the bathroom and scream that *we needed a priest, we needed a priest. There's rapping on the walls.*

When I got to Louise's room, the blanket was pulled up to her chin, her small-set eyes fearfully wide. Her finger shook as she pointed to the window. Moisture on the glass had formed into Saint Grit's symbol, the jagged branches and curved horn, the condensation slowly fading. "It's there again. Something bad, bad for this whole goddamn town. It's a wicked symbol."

Louise put her hand down at her side, hacking. She looked sunken in, unclean. She looked like her neck would snap in half. "Do one of your spells. For me. This pain is dreadful."

I moved across the bedroom and opened the window. "It's an oven in here," I said. "No wonder you can't breathe. Besides, spells won't help you now."

Louise blinked, taking a sip of water. "Do you want me to die like this? I see you. Going out into the woods. Casting your spells. The trees shake. That ceiling fan pounds!" She moaned, the effort to sit vertically failing her. "You could help me—help us."

"You don't know what you're talking about," I said.

"Did you do that to Hatch? Did you—kill him?" I stood beside her, the oxygen tank ticking into life. She repeated the question. "I always suspected," Louise said.

"Be grateful," I said, reaching into my jeans pocket; a small tin that looked like a locket. "This is manchineel poison. Touch the stuff and your skin would boil. Keep it up, Louise, and I might do just that."

I turned off the light and left her in the dark.

CHAPTER 6.

CASSIDY FLIPPED OFF the radio in the '72 Chevy. Fresh tree stumps lined the outskirts of the quiet road looking like gray leading edges of UFOs under a flank of stars. Cows and goats grazed in the high grass, covered in flies and fleas. The cold front had lifted in Sugar Bends and the air was rich with sun-rot, smelling of skunk in Briggs Valley.

"Do you remember a peculiar old woman that played a horn at the farm?" I asked, flicking my cigarette butt out the window. "She wore a bonnet. My father would drive us out here to get milk and butter. Milk was still distributed in glass jars. She'd beckon me to stand next to her at the fence while my brothers petted the goats."

Cassidy took her eyes off the road. She checked her blue eye shadow in the mirror. "I don't remember a lady with a horn. No wonder this place got shut down; gave everybody the creeps."

"There wasn't anything to be afraid of."

We parked at the half-mile marker to the water tower near a row of electrical pylons. Lovebugs had smashed their mating carcasses into the fender on the way up. Our coven friends, men and women, congregated in filthy hemmed robes smoking weak grass, standing in red buckeye and sun-bleached grass. The field was vast and treeless except for the deep wood in the distance. It was still a quiet affair, the coven. We didn't speak of it when we saw each other in town. The women seemed to stare at me a beat longer than the men, like they suspected my sinister intentions to find a man to give me daughters, to give me a son to sacrifice, to gain the trust of my friends if only to obliterate them to feed the poisonous land they danced upon like it was theirs. It was not theirs.

Twenty of us joined hands in a circle without a fire, some of the men barefoot. The black rain from across town made a healthy bonfire almost impossible this time of year. Two men (one of whom I presumed Cassidy was sleeping with based on her flushed expression when she saw him trot down the reeds) emerged from a red barn with a single lightbulb shining off the eaves. They carried with them a red wagon without wheels, heavy and awkward. The men heaved the wagon to the edge of our circle, lifting white cloths from their delicate positions, unwrapping sharp daggers; silver, tarnished, old like a Halloween prop. They kissed Cassidy, one at a time, and gave her two daggers held at arm's length skyward as if in generous offering.

"A gift to you, Goddess, for providing us with the four elements; earth, air, water, fire. We ask you to keep our circle safe from dark spirits. We ask you for guardianship. Let us help the ones that cannot help themselves; the incarcerated, the homeless, the—"

"The marrieds," one of the men giggled, the man who helped carry the red wagon and made doe-eyes at Cassidy.

I was restless of this coven, of Cassidy and her irrevocably performative drawing down the moon, lifting the dagger to kiss the blade, pointing it north. She did the same with the other dagger, pointing it south. She was a distraction to the darker things I was capable of, to the witch inside of me. The two men took the daggers from her and placed them at the edges of the circle, four separate ritualized points—their elements they were so fond of—and with the final dagger, dipped it into a goblet of red wine, pointing east. The funny man held the goblet and gulped the wine afterward.

"You need blood," I said, breaking the silence. "You can't use wine."

Everybody looked at me, the women especially miffed. Cassidy smiled. "Nadine," she said. "It's just ceremonial."

"It's pageantry," I said. I could feel the eyes of the funny man on me, looking me up and down lustfully as he walked through the circle to stand with his friends.

"She's got claws," the funny man said, and the men chuckled.

Cassidy sighed, irritated that I'd broken her concentration. "Next time we'll skin a pig and bury it east, how's that?"

Under a coal-dark night, everybody danced, brightening the mood. Two women played a banjo drum and ukulele, stomping their feet in the grass. All of us in our robes alternating hips and ritualized stepping in the summer heat. I didn't find the dancing rousing or imaginative. If Cassidy was my first sacrifice, where would I go to perform the ritual? Perhaps the woods behind the house. Maybe somewhere else entirely. Not here.

Something caught my eye far off in the distance by the goats behind the fence. I left the dancing circle and approached the small dip in the dirt and grass. Moths hummed around shadow light by the red barn. I wondered if that was where the horn lady used to play, used to beckon me while Hatch and Davey played with the animals, while my father paid for the milk in a glass jar.

"Hope you weren't disappointed there's no bonfire," a man said, coming up behind me from the valley.

The funny man. It was the first unshaded look I got of this man's face as he ambled up the barn path. I felt a pang of lust shoot through my thighs and ribcage like electricity. I knew then: He would be a gift to Saint Grit. He would not live to be an old man. He would die under my thumb.

"You're asking for it; walking this way by yourself," he said.

"My name's Nadine Boone," I said.

"Elliot Walker." He was tall with a flop of dark hair and mustache, looking more 1970s than 1980s, but looking like all the other working men in this town. He was handsome, freckled with a deep voice.

"Elliot Walker," I said. "I don't need a bonfire. I'd roast like a marshmallow in this heat."

Elliot laughed. "So, you're a bloodhound. I find drinking blood upsets the spirits, that's why I always opt for red wine. It's hard finding people south of the Bible Belt that enjoy skyclad ceremonial magic."

"Is that what I have to look forward to? You and the boys running around naked fetching wagons for Goddess Cassidy?"

Elliot basked in the way I spoke to him. He accepted it as flirtation and a man like him that relied on my deferential submission didn't question things, not anything that wasn't actively oppressing him. A man like Elliot wasn't wondering what I was doing out by the fence with the goats looking in the grass at what caught my eye.

"Alright," Elliot said. "You say ritual nudity is for the birds, and I say drinking or offering blood is for the birds. Do you believe in the power of ceremonial magic?"

"Black mass," I said. "A woman needs a coven."

"Black mass?" Elliot laughed. "Are you a Satanist?"

"I'm a solitary witch."

"Lucky for you, Nadine Boone, I find witches better company than Methodists."

I caught a glimpse of a dead snake in the grass, brown and yellowed scales like rubber in a bed of earthworms. Maggots squirmed in and out of its gaping mouth. Its body was lethally gigantic. Must've eaten a deer or a coyote.

"Hey, that's a Burmese python," Elliot exclaimed, narrowing his gaze. "What the hell's that doing out here?"

I approached the python in the grass, the other half of its dead weight wrapped around the dented fence. I unfurled it tenderly, picking it up. It was cold to the touch. It was cold like the manchineels behind the house. It looked like Davey's old pet snake.

Elliot backed away from me as I examined the dead

thing in my hands. "Pythons are like vipers. I wouldn't touch that. You'll piss out venom or something."

A gift, like the symbols, the totem in the black rained soil.

"She's beautiful," I said. "Didn't you hear what I said, Elliot? I said she's beautiful. Don't be bashful. We're the predators. She's dead anyhow, you've nothing to be afraid of."

Elliot shivered, hugging himself. "I don't like snakes."

She was draped over my shoulder and down my chest, dragging the dead python in the grass as Elliot and I walked back to the coven with our backs pressed against the darkness. "Saw something like that in the Everglades once. She probably tried to eat a goat."

"You shouldn't bite off more than you can chew," I said satisfactorily. "It takes a python days to digest a deer, much less a human. She's heavy."

"Have you ever seen anything like it? It's repulsive. It's serpentine!"

"All the gifts I'm given are cold," I said.

Elliot looked me up and down holding this python, again, unquestioning, horny, lightening up. "What's it feel like?" he asked.

I beamed at Elliot and then the python, as if I was holding our firstborn. "She feels smooth. She ate something she wasn't supposed to. I wouldn't suggest you touch her, even if she is dead."

Elliot laughed, enjoying me. The subject of death and his small version of black magic didn't bother him. Some men couldn't be bothered to think of things far into the future, even beyond their own existence. Suddenly, the snake seemed as mundane as roadkill on the side of the road to Elliot Walker. The katydids clicked, the night full of stars above sheets of smoke coming from the west.

"Are you a witch, too?" I asked.

"No," he said, his hands stuffed in his pockets. "Spell magic, prayer, I don't mind it much. I gallivant up here every month just like I do the Methodist church. Being out here in the valley is refreshing; witches and pagans don't mind the heat. This is just the law of attraction. Probably a nifty type of physics if I ever got around to reading about the stuff. I'm a little of this, a little of that."

We walked around the barn, the distant laughter from the coven playing across the vast, high grass land. We were alone. I put the python back in the grass.

"Money or love?" Elliot asked.

"Money, of course. Money can't buy everything. You, sir, will give me three daughters."

"Three," Elliot beamed. "Not four? What about five?"

"Three; all girls. One right after the other."

Elliot searched for something to say. I could see it all over him, the need for talking. He removed a fat cigar from his shirt pocket, lit the foot, and the thick smoke waded between us.

"You're not going to offer me some?" I asked.

"This is a man's smoke. No women allowed. You girls have your snakes and the three daughters you've demanded of me, Nadine Boone. I'll give you daughters. But I won't give you a cigar."

We kissed for the first time and I filled him with the scent of oakwood and pine.

Louise died of pneumonia the same winter that Elliot and I got hitched in a small ceremony officiated by Cassidy at Briggs Valley, surrounded by the coven and friends from the tavern. Elliot worked in ten-hour shifts on a forklift at the lumberyard. He came home with the scent of cedar and bourbon on his work denim. He waited for a baby like an infant would appear in a furnished nursery. He stacked dirty dishes around the sink and waited for me to clean them. Elliot didn't have time to take care of things.

"You were gone forever," he said, when I came in from orgasming into the earth.

"Hardly," I said.

Elliot's keen curiosity regarding my rituals was burdened by a quick flaring terror upon seeing fast-moving black shadows on the walls of our drafty second story. We were taking groceries out of the Pinto when Elliot stopped me on the steps. "Open one door, you open all doors, Nadine."

"What are you going on about?"

Elliot gestured to the slash in the trees beyond the cottonweeds and planters. "When you go out there, doing spells by yourself, doesn't mean you can close what you bring in."

I shifted the weight of the paper bag into my other arm. "You sound afraid, Elliot."

"I'm not afraid. I'm bothered. I'm worried about what's out there."

But I needed Elliot to trust me and our marriage and my private rituals, even if that meant spending more time with him than he deserved. I quit attending the coven. I quit going to Briggs Valley altogether, finding the time spent with other women strange and difficult, for they never expressed the same desires that I did; power over the land and in sex. They wanted new age and camaraderie, prayer and games.

At the start of our marriage, in the early spring of 1985, Elliot and I went on double-dates with Donna and Ted, sometimes Cassidy and her new beau, Isaac. We drove up to Briggs Valley and drank in low-lit tables backdropped with purple vinyl chairs and loveseats at a cocktail lounge called The Merit, the first of its kind this side of rural farm and swamp. But those dates became less as Elliot became more transfixed with what I'd brought into the house with my spells.

He tore up the attic crawlspace, leaving yellow sheets of insulation exposed. The house was a humid cave after that. He surmised the grim possibility of bats or a colony of wasps creating shadows on the walls, tricking him. He hung his favorite .22 target hunting rifle above the fireplace. He admired the hideous thing like it was a rare painting or family portrait. He seemed to think a weapon would scare away a bad spirit.

Elliot's first glimpse of Saint Grit happened while we were screwing. He fucked hard and fast like all men who are poor in bed fuck, and on this night, in the dark, he moaned. He didn't usually moan when he was inside of me. His weight pressed into my hips as he thrusted forward, watching my tits underneath him. I saw the change in his eyes as soon as he saw the witch. He felt her, at first, what I could only imagine was like patches of sea grass crawling down his back. He blinked rapidly, still inside of me, looking up at the pink headboard.

"What the hell was that?" he said.

He froze in stark terror. I could see her leafy, bunched reflection in his hazel eyes, jagged tree branches, wildly vined into my hair like seaweed, and a luminous row of monster teeth as she looked straight into Elliot. Elliot pulled out of me, screaming, falling off the bed.

"What—what the fuck was that? Nadine, what the fuck was that?!"

"You're getting hysterical."

"Nadine—"

Elliot huffed, sweat beading his upper lip. "Somebody was here. A woman."

I jolted out of bed, joining him on the floor. I felt a wet heat on my back. I glanced toward the bed. The vines were gone. She was gone. She was safe inside of me, still growing.

"There was a witch," Elliot panted. "She had big teeth. She was in bed with us."

I comforted my husband. I held him closely and told him that it was going to be alright, that the shadows of the southern oak trees had scared him.

"You really shouldn't drink so much," I said. "Look how it's affecting you."

Saint Grit was having an effect on all of Sugar Bends, not just our shanty house. We had snow flurries before the spring harvest, subsequent to brushfires that spiked out of nowhere on the side of the roads and in the cemetery, even below the low fieldstone to the lighthouse. The totem, that I so graciously kept private and tenderly cared for, seemed to get more bones around it all the time in the curve of the goat's horn. I took the bones from the sacred little space in the totem and laid them out in the soil under the manchineel; a tiny talus and a kneecap split in two like an animal skull. I buried the bones under leaves until it was time to gather more and put them there.

Elliot's disdain for witchcraft grew stronger after my miscarriage. He punched a hole in the drywall by the stack of firewood ten weeks into a failed pregnancy. He couldn't look at me, not even while a pink yolky sac floated in black blood at the bottom of the toilet. Elliot refused to mop the linoleum and bath mat stained with what gushed out of me. He sent for Cassidy to wipe the bloody lumps off the floor.

I was not relieved for Cassidy's company. She'd shown interest in wanting to see the manchineels up close, unafraid of their poisons because Elliot disclosed that I performed spells around the trees. She wanted to see what the fuss was about.

"Nadine," she said, the next morning after I bled all over the bathroom and sat in a healthy nest of blankets on the porch. It was May. The black smoke rose again, the air thick and fragrant in turpentine. "There's something, like a twig, sticking out of your ankle."

My abdomen was in agony, knotted and sore, but I bent forward in the rocking chair to peel the thin lip of a manchineel leaf, embedded in my skin in thin layers. Fresh blood came, brittle and dry as if preserved in a book. Cassidy blinked, her once trusting face now matching that of Elliot's fear. There was an indent where I pulled leaves from out of my body.

"Guess tick season is early this year." I smiled.

Every summer night after that, Elliot returned home from the lumberyard tasting of another woman's oils, salty and milky-sweet. Cassidy, of course. The infidelity would work in my favor soon. Cassidy, the ultimate offering to not just Saint Grit, but to the town. I never desired anything other than my own self-pleasure and it was about to come to fruition.

The summer of 1985 the town, although employed, was nervous. Sugar Bends had troubled skies and symbols still marking up the high school and the gas station pumps. The men were getting sick. Townies called it the Bends Disease. Men were getting the Bends Disease, showing up to work with flu-like symptoms, unfocused, mesmerized by the trees, fucking up on the jobs, sitting at changed traffic lights staring off into space while car horns blared. They suffered screaming night terrors. Everybody noticed.

I sat with Donna at Hunky Dory's diner like we used to do when we were teenagers after school. We shared a mound of buttery pancakes and black coffee. "Ted's sick with that male flu," she said. "I don't know what to do anymore."

I shrugged. "*Reader's Digest* says more than half the population will suffer from seasonal allergies by 1990."

"He coughs all night. Doctor says his lungs are clear, maybe it's a side effect of the burnings but Ted's never had a problem before. I went outside and he dropped to his knees, hypnotized by a pine tree. I don't know, kid, I'm worried about all of the men in this town."

I dropped my fork, gazing out the windows. Other diner patrons did the same thing, standing from their booths or the counter to watch. A row of men outside on the sidewalk looked skyward with their arms down at their sides, as if waiting to be taken by a distant ship.

"Nadine, what is it? What's out there?" Donna said.

SAINT GRIT

For a moment, I, too, was worried, but it faded into a smile as I felt Saint Grit's skeleton move within mine.

I couldn't stay pregnant in 1985, and Elliot took it upon himself to suggest we spend time in nature away from the trees, away from the house where he'd stopped going upstairs because of the rapping on the walls. He slept on the couch instead, afraid of the floor-to-ceiling shadows. Elliot seemed to know that I did not need him, but I needed him for something. It showed on his face.

CHAPTER 7.

WE SAT UP naked in bed, drinking Pabst Blue Ribbon. I asked Elliot to light my cigarette. "Something funny happened today," I said.

"Yeah?"

"You know that hardware store with the Halloween masks? I went in and picked one out today."

Elliot flipped on the T.V. and switched the channels until he got to Johnny Carson. He turned up the volume. "Why'd you do that?"

"Put it on for me, Elliot?" I smiled, closing the bed sheet around my body. "I've got it hanging in the closet."

"What for?"

"Come on, it'll be fun. I want to see what you look like in it."

Elliot sighed playfully. He pulled on his underwear and walked to the closet. "It's a devil's mask."

"Yes, that's the one."

"Nadine—"

It was a standard Halloween mask; a devil face. It was plastic and red with two white horns sticking out from the top and a grimacing oval-white mouth. The eyes were painted black.

"What am I supposed to do with this?" Elliot flicked the string in the back. "Thought you wanted to watch Carson."

I grabbed the bedside ashtray, exhaling. "Won't you just do what I ask you?"

Elliot scoffed. "You're something else sometimes." He put the devil's mask on. "There. Happy?"

"No. I don't like it on you. Take it off and never put it on again."

Elliot turned off the T.V. He kept the mask on, and took the cigarette out of my hand. "You go out there and find yourself in the woods drawn to everything except for me."

"I just wanted to see what you looked like in it."

"I'm not so sure," Elliot said.

He pulled me to the edge of the bed. He lifted the devil's mask up to his forehead as I pushed his head down between my legs so he would lick and suck the softest parts of me. I felt the surge of climax just as Elliot lifted his face and wiped his mouth with the back of his hand.

"What are you doing?" I said.

Elliot smiled, snapping the mask back on his face, fucking me until he was done. When he pulled out, he tossed me the mask, and walked naked into the bathroom.

"You fucked with my orgasm, Elliot," I said, retrieving the Halloween mask from the sheets.

Elliot pissed with the door open. He looked over his shoulder. "What are you getting at?"

"I *said* you fucked with my orgasm."

Elliot spit into the toilet. "You're going to go fuck with your trees anyway, Nadine. Go out there and get it if you want it. Come on, you had a good time."

I walked for two days straight after that without stopping other than to pick lantanas from the ferns. I whistled as I went, not needing sleep or food or a break off my feet. The mangroves' branches sagged, giving off a sinister look when I walked by. I watched the school children pour out of the bus carrying bright orange sacks of candy. Some of the children were in costume even though Halloween wasn't until tomorrow. I stopped at the edge of the sidewalk where two boys dressed in drugstore vampire costumes gasped when they saw me. The one boy looked down at my feet.

"Let's get the heck out of here," the kid said, and they were off.

As I continued down Marsten Street toward Tidioute, I realized they'd heard my footfalls; like a giant stepping through leaf-fallen concrete. Saint Grit was picking up her pace inside of me. I smelled of the earth now, wet soil and grass.

I took my time through the woods to Briggs Valley, walking along the crabgrass and juniper buckeye, the smell of hot grass greasing the air. Roger was there looking sickly and unclean, his hair matted around his neck like a dog with mange.

"Who's there?" Roger said, perking up from the grass. He had a backpack with him and he clutched it to his chest. "I said, 'who's there?'"

I strolled out of the sagebrush whistling.

"Stay away from me. Stay away," he cried, noticing my fingernails like talons. He closed his eyes, his jaw shaking. "I've dreamed of you every night for—"

"A lust that cannot be relieved," I said, towering over him. "I've invaded your dreams since high school."

"Go away. Please, let me be."

I noticed his body, his skin was filthy, pocked in goose flesh. He'd been outside and exposed to the elements for a long time. Roger lifted his head from the corner of his backpack, squinting from a sunbeam. He put his palm up to see clearer. "Get away from me, you witch. I told the sheriff about you. I told the school kids to watch out."

"How did you get that?" I asked.

He brought his trembling hands up to his jaw and stuck out his tongue where plump, oozing-infected boils were as red as fresh tomatoes. "It hurts," he mumbled. "It hurts to talk."

"I'll see you around, Roger. Happy Halloween."

I went about my walk through the grass, listening to my footfalls and whistling.

CHAPTER 8.

THE SOUND OF the ancient horn came like an asteroid from the belly of the valley where wet moss and reeds were tangled among snarls of crabgrass. I stood at the edge of the dairy farm by a cement drinking trough. I was surrounded by hollow wooden barrels turned over on their sides while six teenage girls were down on all fours, with their heads stuffed into the former skins of farm goats with smooth, leather-twined horns and floppy black ears. I, too, wore a goat's head like a mask, having slaughtered the animals with a machete, using a bone saw to cut through the jaw, teeth, midline, and brain. Where the eyes had been sunken, turning yellowish. A fine tuft of black fur hung from the angular chin, mangy with blood. It took hours to gut the insides but I was efficient because Saint Grit made me that way.

Above my lip, inside the mask, it smelled like rot.

This was the ritual under a full moon, full dark night during an unremitting heatwave in the summer of 1986. The girls believed I was saving them from the Bends Disease when it came for them—if it ever would—that they'd get free of the toxic men in their life if they just helped me with this one thing. They could do whatever they wanted out here, I told them when I recruited them from the sidewalks near their school or jobs; no fear, no judgment. Nobody would catch them foraging on their darkest desires.

Cassidy was in the pasture, pleading for mercy. They'd

eaten her hair, ripped it from her skull and pawed at the blond strands while standing on her abdomen. She had violent black smudges on her jawline as she'd braced for impact, missing. I'd knocked out two fillings from her canines. The girls chomped her hair in Cassidy's ear, slurping, licking their chops.

When the Chevy rumbled up the wooded path, I ordered my goats to stay low in the grass. "Leave Cassidy be," I said, like she was a sleeping dog.

I disappeared into the barn watching Elliot cut the engine and look for me in the sleepy valley, the shadow of the water tower shading his confused expression. He didn't see me in the doorway of the barn. A cowardly man, I thought, watching him hike up the grass and jump the fence. He spit, picking up a fern and putting it dry in his mouth.

"Nadine?" he called, frogs croaking. "Who's there? I'm too tired for games."

He spit the fern out, gazing over the valley. Too dark to see but it was where we first met. I knew I had him when he caught sight of me standing in the doorway, although he didn't know it was me. He saw somebody standing there with a realistic goat's mask over their face, dressed in black. I watched his face turn crestfallen, his eyes return to the Chevy with the open driver's door, deciding if he should run back to the truck.

"Get him, goats," I ordered, and his eyes rose in recognition at the sound of my voice behind the mask.

The girls were upon him, coming out of the grass like strange beasts.

Elliot collapsed into the grass. I joined the girls as they made chomping noises at him, smelling the aroma of alfalfa and huskseed on their breath. I smelled like I'd just come out of the pasture, as though I *was* the pasture, the land, and had been for hundreds of years.

The girls put their hands primally on Elliot, pulling at his hair, his clothes, his skin. I could see him mouth, "Nadine", but no sound came as they were upon him.

My eyes gleamed sharply at Cassidy, who bled and moaned by herself in the pitch black. I walked toward her, with heavy footfalls, tracing my fingertips along the smooth horns. Most of her left arm had been eaten off, the humerus hanging off the shoulder in two split pieces. I looked in the grass until I found the other half of her arm— the ulna—jellied with thick tissue and blood, veins that could still be seen like punctured flames. I picked up the ulna and prodded her ribcage with it.

"Come on, Cassidy," I said. "Up we go."

She begged, drooling alfalfa and dirt, blood.

I guided her up the hemlock with her own arm, prodding her to climb, keep climbing. She cried hysterically, pulling herself up the twisted branch. Her pants were torn. The branch shook. I prodded her in the half-boned socket of her left side. The ground was pooled in blood. "Keep up," I said. She pushed and the lichen covered her legs, her face, thickly knotting around her forehead. She hyperventilated, going into shock as the lichen branch turned her upside down where she watched Elliot get rolled into a barrel across the wooded path. I took the goat's horn from my head as I climbed the tree. I slammed the goat's horn into her rectum as her large intestine opened and spilled, gutted from the inside out. I took the other horn from my head and forced it down her throat, teeth flew out at me and blood, and by the time I got the horn into her mouth, she was dead.

Elliot lunged for the barn, but a goat seized his waist and another goat smashed the sole of his work boot. The fresh pain made him scream. I climbed down the tree and met my husband in the pasture, hitting him across the face. I dragged him by his long hair back toward the barrel that he ran from. The goats pawed at alfalfa, stuffing it into his mouth as he choked. He could not flail with the other goats on top of him. He tried lashing with his feet, his lower half, but they were as hard as iron, and his eyes were pocked with specks of dirt.

"It burns!" he screamed.

The goats slurped viciously in his ear.

I took my favorite devil's mask from my robe and slipped it around his skull as the goats stuffed more pasture into his mouth. His clothes were soaked and I smelled the acrid smell of urine, the back of his neck was wet. The echo of his respiration went in and out rapidly.

"Get the barrel," I said.

We rolled Elliot into the grass. Out of the eye holes, I imagined him looking at the goats, these girls, emerging out of the thick, knee-high weeds. He could certainly make out the outline of the others' twisted horns pointing toward the black sky. Half-dressed. One girl was naked and swam through the grass toward him, her breasts hanging like moons. Two girls, one of them pregnant, grabbed long sticks and tools, thrashing the pasture around him.

Engulfed in darkness, I wanted Elliot to see the whites of their eyes. This animal hunger, so piercing, razor wire to his soul. In perfect unison, the goats dropped to all fours, feeding him blades of grass, making wet, apocalyptic noises at him.

"Put him inside," I ordered, and one of the goats grabbed a shovel, filling the barrel's hollow chamber with grass.

The goat-masked beasts rolled Elliot onto his back, lifted, and pushed, sealing him into the barrel with a round, rain-slicked lid. The birds came and then the rain.

It rained for days after our valley ritual. I could still hear Elliot's primal groaning and cries of anguish as I drove out of Sugar Bends and on I-10. Putting distance between myself and the woods and the valley was in my best interest, at least for a few days. My coven girls needed cooling off. They wanted more from me, wanted something more lurid even after all that play in the woods—hadn't I indulged them enough? Women of a certain age are always starving and I'm unwilling to give it. "Conjure your own," I told a girl, as I locked up the Suwanee Rd. house and peeled out like a bat out of hell. I didn't need the coven girls anymore. Maybe I never did.

I drove to the Alabama border and checked myself into a motel with a hybrid gas station and 24-hour diner. I made appearances at meal times after local news flashed Cassidy Burke's face on the T.V. *Mill worker's body was found dumped on the side of the road in Sugar Bends . . . "* I sipped stale, overroasted coffee as the waitress came by, shaking my head at what this world was coming to. I gestured to the corner of the ceiling at the T.V.

"How does something like that happen?" I said.

She looked over her shoulder and made a sigh of indignation, putting a plate of grilled cheese and soup in front of me that I wasn't hungry for. "Beats me. Some low-lifes did that to her. You bring people into this world that don't wanna be here, I guess."

"What was she doing out there by herself anyway?" I said. "Asking for it."

"Maybe a creep pulled her into the woods."

Maybe, maybe, maybe. Everybody wanted a maybe because it was easier than the darkness invading the town. Saint Grit's leaves and rain purged our fingerprints.

After dinner and a stroll in the backroads that lasted for days, no exhaustion had set in and I bought a pregnancy test and pissed on the plastic strip under a full moon. (The coven girls would've had a field day with that endeavor.) I returned to the motel room and the bathroom mirror above the sink shattered as two blue lines appeared in tandem.

I was pregnant. I could begin.

CHAPTER 9.

A MAN STIRS in the grass with his cheek pressed against a triangle of moss that's crested the underside of a fox hole. He's near a sewer drain and the rainwater that trickles in wakes him fully. His face is sunburned. It's August and sweltering heat. He leans up on his elbows, watching cows graze and chickens run to the corner of their pen where an old woman feeds them.

The man perceives her as somebody he knows but can't place, not his wife, but somebody that has taken care of him in this pasture for days at a time, maybe weeks, maybe longer. She's dressed in layers of rags, sewn together and barely held together with loose threads.

He is afraid of her.

Ravens glide in and around the sky, diving down into the moss and skyward again. Their cawing startles him as the old woman walks slowly toward him. She has gray hair pinned beneath a floral bonnet. She is wearing his old work boots—at least, he thinks they once belonged to him—and they're unlaced. She doesn't make eye contact with him, lassoing him like an animal. She pulls it and he doesn't nudge. She does it again and he gives in, remembering. This happened yesterday, too. And the day before that. For a long time now.

He walks behind her on all fours through the grass and up the mossy crest, into the farm with the cows. The goats are gone, and this he knows. He remembers that, too. He wonders how long the old woman has taken care of him.

He wonders where his wife is, what happened to the house. He can't remember the name of the blue-collar town with the pylons and the bar, all the drinking he did there, the sound of his truck rambling up Devil's Hill.

The old woman ties the rope to the fence. He stays in the patch of grass he's grazed in for days, starving. He can smell his own ripe body odor. He can't remember smelling anything that awful in his life. He doesn't talk because his mouth is too dry. There's blades of grass caked into his tongue and the sound of his own voice is hard to hear.

Suddenly, he remembers the bad part. The bad things that happen here.

He squirms, looking for a way out. He watches the old woman pick up an ancient-looking horn made from an enclosed shell. He mumbles, spitting out blades of grass. He can't protest. He is too weak. She plays the notes: they are harsh and like a blowhorn. It rings in his ears. The trees in the wood tremble and shake, losing their branches as they sag to one side. The horn bleats as she approaches him. He remembers how he's fed, how he's stayed alive this long. Tomorrow it will be the same.

She pours scalding brimstone down his throat, scalding his insides. He bleats throughout the day and into the night.

CHAPTER 10.

I NAMED OUR firstborn daughter Pippa Agnes Boone. She turned five years old having never met Elliot because Elliot was still being taken care of in the barn by the old witch at the farm. I took Pippa to see him sometimes, to pet the goats. One night, after dusk, Pippa and I laid animal bones in the triangle next to the manchineel tree with our lanterns dimmed down. Saint Grit left them for me to find every morning in the corner of the house, in the living room fireplace, up the stairs, at the foot of Pippa's bed; bones, usually from a small animal. We gathered soil from the edges of the trees and buried the bones where fungus hemmed the bottom of flower pots filled with rainwater and manchineel sap.

The house on Suwanee Road was crawling with sharp vines and tree moss, rooting from the ground up. It had been this way for a very long time.

I was in the kitchen when I heard the Chevy rumble down the road and turn into the drive. Pippa demanded who it was, running to the window to see the man who came tumbling through the front door like a ragged scarecrow.

"There you are," I said cheerfully. "Welcome back."

Elliot walked with a hunch wearing clothes that were too big for him, his eyes narrowed and tired and his face and body dirty.

I lit one of his cigars, taking a long, warm inhale. "How was your workday?"

Pippa approached him, gently placing a small hand on his shoulder. "We came to see you sometimes. Did you like it?"

Elliot was breathless, gesturing for water. He looked around him expecting water to come out of a spicket ready for him to lick up. He slumped back into the armchair, a sad, sinister look in his eyes, knowing I'd taken charge of everything that happened to him, what he could remember of it.

"I have wonderful news," I said. "I'm pregnant again; another girl."

The second baby came that winter, Junia Calliope Boone. I grimaced at this writhing pink creature that the nurse placed on my chest. I was resentful as the nurse pulled my hospital gown down, telling me the baby needed to latch right away. I didn't love Junia, like I didn't love Pippa, but I'd pretend to love both of them. Pretending wasn't difficult. Elliot wasn't in the room when Junia was born. He refused to see my body like that, torn open, my tits doubled in size, serving a purpose other than his own pleasure.

At some point, everybody left me alone with Junia. I took her into the bathroom with me, looking down ruthlessly at this needy thing. All I had to do was give her one hard squeeze and she'd quit breathing, my coven severed.

"I'm Nadine. I'm your mommy," I said.

In the pocket of my robe, I fished out the mint tin where I'd collected the manchineel sap. "Here," I said, cradling her in one hand with her head gently propped into the cushion of my arm—just yesterday still in my body—I rubbed the sap over my nipple. I dipped my finger into the white poison and smeared it across Junia's chin.

"Highest embodiment of human life. Roost, roost with me."

The nurse appeared in the doorway of the bathroom.

I startled, dropping my tin of poison in the sink. I

gripped Junia tightly, giggling, trying to play it off. "Goodness gracious, you frightened me."

The nurse frowned. "Everything alright in here?"

"Remarkable," I said. "I was just saying a little prayer."

The nurse looked at the dripping finger, and I wiped the sap onto my robe. "You should be in bed. I can get you a bedpan." She reached out to me as if to pull my arm away from my infant, to drag me back to the hospital bed. A sharp twist of electricity voltaged between us. The floor seemed to move. The nurse gasped, retreating from the bathroom.

"Next time," I said. "Ask me before you touch me, dear."

CHAPTER 11.

PIPPA AND JUNIA were still children in the summer of 1994, mirror images of Elliot and I, long-haired and scabby-kneed, inherently trusting of me when shadows rapped on the walls and dead leaves showed up on the porch at the crack of dawn. One morning after a brutal storm, the girls were awake and restless, still in bed. It was too early to get up and too late to go back to sleep. The girls were eager. Today we'd take a joy ride through the Florida backcountry.

I floated above the girls' beds secretly, a stranger to gravity in these days when the gift of a deep and dreamless sleep was foreign to me. All I had to do was close my eyes and Saint Grit moved me. At first, it was through the woods, as if I'd never gone to bed at all the night before and had fallen asleep around the planters of bones and charred branches in the triangle. The girls did not know I was in their bedroom.

Pippa peeled back the blinds and unlatched the window lock. She searched the yard from the window, looking for the bull gator she swore she saw slinking from the gurgling reeds after the storm. Unlikely, a gator, but I'd played shocked to give Elliot something to gripe about.

"Pippa," Junia whispered, still nestled under a blanket. They still slept with stuffed animals.

"What?"

"I farted."

"Drop dead."

The girls and I were bright-eyed on the drive. Junia, especially charmed by an Anything Can Happen Day, sitting in the hot Pontiac with a peanut butter and grape jelly sandwich in one hand, a canteen on her hip. We listened to a cassette of Blind Willie Johnson, songs about soul trouble and faith in a Christian god. I liked the steady rhythm of the banjo, a sweet accompaniment to the spiky, overgrown scrubland on either side of us. Pippa didn't say much on the drive. She seemed to understand there was more to the trees to me than just being one with nature. Being a wild, ethereal feminine chanter who did spellwork wasn't cutting it for Pippa—not anymore. She asked if we could go somewhere where there weren't any trees at all.

"I don't know of a place," I said. "Kansas, maybe."

Pippa breathed on the window. "I get tired of it—the trees."

I glanced in the rear view at her, then looked at my reflection. My eyes were turning a shade darker. "I think you'll like where I'm taking you."

"It's hot back here," Junia said. "Can we get out?"

"Not yet," I said. "The Seminoles used to give birth in the sand and then go back to chicken rearing. You'll live."

We turned into farm country north of Ocala, seventy miles out from the sleepy mill-and-lumber corner of Sugar Bends that hung like a barnacle in the distance. The sky turned to watercolor and the citrus trees and bismark palms ceased out in the middle of nowhere. There was a beautiful loom about the pine flatwoods and the occasional mossed-broomed live oak. I drove into a groove of a palmetto bed facing the marshes of a shady wetland, where curling, green lily pads floated on the surface of the gloomy water. I cut the engine. A mist of humidity crept over the water and the Pontiac. The healthy sun was still bright behind us.

"Where are we?" Junia asked.

I turned to the girls with great satisfaction. "You're old enough now that you can handle learning about the coven—our coven."

Pippa frowned, feeling the sun in her lap. Junia's face lit up.

"Your mama's come nose-to-nose with a few men in her day. Men are dangerous creatures," I said.

"What's that mean?" Junia asked.

"Let her talk," said Pippa.

"But she is talking."

"Put a lid on it!"

"Quiet, girls," I snapped. I rolled the window down, taking a cigarette from the glove compartment. "Your father made me keep the secrets about the coven from you. That alone keeps me in a minefield, a wormhole."

Pippa unstuck her thigh from the seat, exchanging glances with Junia.

"He's doom and gloom, your dad. Your dad, too, is a man and therefore a dangerous creature. The Bends Disease is getting to him."

"My teacher says it's environmental," Pippa said.

I laughed. "Environmental. Do you believe that?"

"I don't know." She shrugged.

"Is Dad one of the sick ones, too?" Junia said.

I exhaled cigarette smoke in their little angel faces. They were used to it. The smell of tobacco was warm as I flicked the ash. "I'm not immune to men communicating in mumbles and unexpected bursts of violence. You won't be soon enough either. That's what the coven is for. A safe place to be wild and free. Do you understand?"

"What about Dad?" Junia asked.

"Dad's a myth, my dear," I said. "So is fatherhood. Men are myths. I brought you into this world with my own trees. Danger—that's what men have brought into Sugar Bends."

Pippa cringed, looking on the verge of tears. "You're making this up."

"Perhaps," I said. "But I think you know better."

Pippa looked out the window.

"Your father is repulsive to me. He calls me names. Bad names only angry men call women. It started not long after he visited an old witch that lives below the water tower in Briggs Valley. She plays a horn made out of shell, and one day, when you're old enough, you'll hear her horn blow, and then it's time to go—the three of us. Saint Grit lives inside of me and the old witch is helping her grow; she gives us bones and leaves in return, preservations of the earth. It's primitive."

"What about school?" Junia said.

"When you hear the horn, you won't care about school anymore," I said. "Saint Grit gave me a totem before either of you were born. I buried it under the manchineel trees. The old witch has been back for a long time."

"You told us the old woman was a farmer," Pippa said.

"She is a farmer of ancient things," I said. "Chin up. We're protecting you from the evil that men do."

Suddenly, rising out of the craggy flatwoods was a gray ring of smoke. There was nobody out here but us. I asked the girls to join me through the marsh and into the forest. Pippa protested but gave up instantly as Junia was racked with cries about staying alone in the hot car. Our shoes were soaked, sidestepping the wetland as our legs got bitten and red in the terrible heat. We arrived at a square clearing in the middle of the pine flatwoods. I knelt down at the burning, smelly gift. It was rotten.

"What stinks?" Junia said.

"A totem." I smiled contemptuously. "We've been gifted, girls. Remember what I told you? Do what thou wilt."

The girls knelt on either side of me. Birds cawed over our heads, fading fast. There was a hemlock branch tied in filthy knots to black-spotted leaves that kindled in whipping flames out of a moist sack of human molars. The was a nest made out of moss and a dense, bloodied ovary cradling the edges of human toes peppered with splinters.

Pippa gasped, holding her knees against her chin. She dropped her head down. Junia grabbed onto her sister and whimpered.

"This belonged to a woman I knew before you were born," I said. I fingered the bloody crevices of the moss-sack. "Her name was Cassidy Burke. We worked together. We were friends. And she was your father's lover before this happened to her."

"No!" Pippa said. "Don't tell us this! I want to go back to the car and go home!"

Junia tried taking her sister's hand, standing with her in a solidarity she didn't understand. I winked at Junia, just to soften her mood, pulling blades of grass up from the ground and twirling it between my index finger.

"It's going to be alright," I said. "You're a girl. And one day you'll understand. You'll hear the horn, too."

"No!" Pippa said.

She went running from the wood and back into the marsh, splashing. I heard the car door slam. Junia looked at me, narrowing her gaze back to the totem.

"Is it real?" Junia asked. "The coven?"

"A mother doesn't lie to her children."

That night back at home, after the temperature dropped and the sky was overcast and the streetlights flooded Suwanee Road, Pippa pretended to be wiped out. Junia joined her and they talked in secret like sisters or friends do. I buried the totem in the woods and eavesdropped in floating-space, defying gravity, unknown to the two of them as they dressed for bed.

"Do you think Mom's telling the truth about dad being mean?" Junia said. She played a Gameboy in bed.

Pippa glanced sharply at her sister, taking her eyes off her Lois Duncan paperback. "You're like Dad if you think Mom's lying."

"I never thought of it like that."

"Don't say stuff like that."

"I won't."

The ceiling fan's chain slapped against the dusty wing. Junia flipped on the night light, asking for ice cream. Pippa said it was too late, but Junia eventually got her way and they crept downstairs, only their white, pointy noses seen in the darkness.

"What's that sound?" Pippa whispered. "Hear it?"

"No."

"Listen."

They looked small in their night clothes. Their footfalls on the cherry wood floorboards.

"What is that?" Junia asked.

"Let's look."

They crept behind the staircase to the mudroom on the other end of the foyer. There was nothing of interest except a flickering lamp, ready to burn out.

"Come on," Pippa said. "It's just that stupid light again."

In the dark, anything seemed possible.

They left the mudroom, turning the corner in zipped-in darkness. Saint Grit appeared at the top of the staircase.

Saint Grit's inverted face dripped in shadows. Her jaw moved languidly exposing a row of all molar teeth. Her triangular head hung below a tree branch that was caked in fungi sores and wet leaves. She bent toward the cries of the girls, growling heinously as the manchineel sap bled out of the curve of her mottled face. Pippa and Junia screamed in horror. Nothing about Saint Grit suggested she was human, or ever was. They could not hear the ancient horn as Saint Grit lunged for them. The horn was still too far away.

CHAPTER 12.

THE BENDS DISEASE worsened when the snow came in January. The last time Florida had snow, I was just a little girl in the early 1970s and our house didn't have heat. Hatch was still alive. Davey seemed like a baby then. This time, the sap on our poison trees froze and the lichen faded white into the bark. I carefully carved out the yellow slime mold and planted it into the ground as an offering until I could get pregnant. The girls were in school, Pippa in sixth grade and Junia in third.

Elliot and Pippa had begun looking at me in pure terror. Sometimes they didn't know I could see them by the Christmas tree light ór in the shower with the curtain shut. Elliot cried in his sleep, suffering nightmares that I'd pretend to awake from. I soothed Elliot, petting his long hair out of his eyes, rocking him back to sleep, if he could ever get back to sleep at all. He dreamt of the old witch night after night; he was a goat again, on all fours, eating pasture, hooked to a chicken pen. He was dehydrated, uncontrollably sweating as his lungs filled with dirt.

Elliot cried with his head in my neck. "She keeps giving me hot coals to swallow. It burns. I wake up and it's like it's real."

"It was only a dream," I said.

I smiled at the reflection of the old witch looking back at me in the mirror across from our bed.

One cold night it snowed again. There was an ice storm north of the Carolinas. It swept south and we had snow flurries graze over our land that looked like shiny hail in the middle of the night. I sprang out of bed when I heard dishes clashing in the kitchen sink. I could see from the top of the stairs the white light from the refrigerator streaking the wooden floors. Glass was getting dunked into the sink and the garbage disposal churned.

Pippa stood at the sink. She wore pajamas with little Coca-Cola pandas on them. The garbage disposal churned and spun. I closed my robe. Lately Pippa had looked at me with a fearful curiosity, but this surprised me. This frantic girl. "What are you doing?" She looked over her shoulder, crying. "Pippa, what are you doing?"

The sink was full of suds. The corners of her eyes crinkled. "Go away!"

She was tossing our food away, everything in the refrigerator. There was open Tupperware and splashes of milk and ketchup on the floor. Elliot and Junia came up behind me.

"What's the racket?" Elliot barked. "It's two o' clock!"

"She won't tell me anything," I said.

I approached the sink where gobs of chicken salad were stuck all over the sink, bread and coffee beans flying up from the overworked disposal. I flipped it off. The refrigerator glowed feebly as I shut the door.

"She's poisoning us!" Pippa said. "She's putting that tree sap in our food and in our drinks! Dad, you've got to believe me!"

Junia ran to her sister, hugging her around the waist.

"Teenage girl blues," I said. "I didn't expect a tantrum."

"Poison?" Elliot said, looking sharply at me. He couldn't find the time to comfort his oldest daughter, but he turned off the sink and wiped his hands on a kitchen towel. "Mama would never poison you."

"Nadine does!"

Junia closed her eyes tightly like a fist. "You're scaring me," she said.

Elliot sighed, kneeling in front of his daughters. They

71

embraced and Pippa looked at me over her father's shoulder. I smiled ruefully at her. *Nadine.*

"I watched her." Pippa sniffed. "She wants to take us into the woods and give us to a demon."

Elliot grabbed Pippa and held her at arm's length. He shook her. "Listen, little girl, don't talk about that garbage in my house!"

"Look, Elliot, now you've made Junia cry, too," I said. "She doesn't look as pretty when she cries."

Elliot let go of Pippa. He pointed his finger at her. "Don't say that *word* again!"

Demon. My daughter was smart but not intelligent.

The girls ran upstairs to bed in blows of hysteria. I cleaned up the mess and tossed out the rest of the food that dripped out of containers and boxes, ignoring Elliot's passive meltdown as he returned to bed. What Pippa couldn't remember from her babyhood were the boils that swelled red and purple on her neck, mistakenly ignored by the town pediatrician as an allergic reaction to the sugarcane burnings. The black rain. The boils would go away on their own. She'd been poisoned long before she could ever remember. Soon she'd hear the horn for the first time.

Almost twenty years ago a man relocated from Sugar Bends to Sedona, far away in the Arizona desert. He was untouched by the Bends Disease: my father, George. He'd spent his time gambling and working in a sporting goods store. I floated to see him that spring, from a cavernous rest that mimicked real sleep. I lifted myself away into darkness, the lonely sound of voices over the Mars-red mesas into a seedy casino where George Boone played a slot machine. He was twenty pounds heavier with a cruddy, tired face. His belly pushed into the coin chute. He shook his plastic cup of coins as he pulled the gold chrome lever.

I waited behind him. I waited for the jaunty jingle of the slot machine to play. Three red stars. He won. Instead of dispensed coins, filthy, wet leaves spit out of the chute. George looked down in bewilderment, calling for a clerk or waitress to help him with this machine. It wasn't fair. He won and now this. Nobody came.

More leaves poured out, but it was the fragrance he recognized. The stink of sun-drenched leaves in a rural Florida town he left ages ago when he was younger and healthier. The same leaves that surrounded his oldest son when he died of—

George felt his stomach tighten, followed by a burning sensation in his chest. I moved his organs. I pushed the organs against each other. He did not know I was there orchestrating his pain, the leaves that gathered in front of him. He sighed, rubbing his chest where it hurt. He didn't bother collecting his winnings and fumbled toward the elevator to his room, where he passed out on the bed.

My father awoke in the town he left back in 1978, but instead of the house by the cemetery he was out by the edge of the woods in a field where the water tower loomed over him strangely. He could hear the distant sound of men's voices as the morning sun shone brightly over the valley. He was on his back, his legs tethered by Saint Grit's leaves, closing in on his body like a swarm of bees. The wet leaves entered his trousers. He gasped, managing to lift himself off the ground, swatting at the leaves.

"Get out of here," he said.

The groans grew closer. Was it one man? Or several? George didn't have the strength to stand. He crawled toward the helpless sound, pawing at the leaves that seemed to vine their way back onto his body.

I watched him like a hawk from a tree, his face turning white as agony filled him upon seeing another man in the grass.

Roger.

Roger hadn't been seen in town for years because he'd

been slowly sinking into the grass, staying alive gnawing on pasture and sipping rainwater.

"Hey mister, what are you doing out here? Can you hear me?" George said.

He choked back a pitiful shriek at the sight in the ground. Roger was engulfed up to his neck in the crabgrass and pine scrub, looking like floating tupelo. He was missing teeth and his lips were bloodied-dry, the edges of his eyes crusted a shade of yellow.

"Please," Roger moaned.

"Mister?"

George surveyed the open field around them.

They were not alone.

There were other men in the grass, their eyes eaten out of the sockets, skulls split open, half-alive with shotgun stares unable to scream.

"Please," Roger said. He'd gone blind in one eye. "For so long . . . here . . . I can't move. Please kill me."

George, too, was sunk into the grass with the other men, and when the full moon came the old witch emerged from the barn and played her ancient horn. She poured brimstone over the soil absorbed in the grass, where the men's tormented wails were lost into the woods. Their hunched wet heads burned from the brimstone and later the sun.

CHAPTER 13.

THE SWIMMING POOL at the Sugar Bends gymnasium off Marsten Road and Placerville hadn't changed much since it opened in the 1950s. It was erected on the corner of the playground across from Phil's Hardware. Even the fiberglass on the pool floor was the same. Elliot swum there in the mornings before the girls got on the bus. One cool autumn morning, I followed him to the parking lot, creeping along the sidewalk and the atrium.

I'd had enough of Elliot and his crass remarks, his lousy strokes during sex.

I quietly went through the gate and walked underneath the bleachers, watching him perform long breaststrokes. He wore a swimmer's cap and goggles that fit too snuggly over his eyes. He couldn't see me. When Elliot reached the other side of the swimming pool, dramatically rising from the water, I emerged from the bleachers giving a flirty wave and admiring his physique as he performed two more laps.

Elliot swam to the edge of the pool where I stood near the mermaid-blue diving board. I knelt down so he could run his wet hand over my thigh and into my underwear, caressing the softness between my legs. I steered his hand up my hip, then abruptly stood gazing wide-eyed into the swimming pool.

"Elliot, did you see that?"

"See what?"

"My earring fell into the water. Look—it's floating to

the bottom; it's my favorite silver piece you got me for Christmas."

Elliot squinted, popping his goggles back on. "You sure?"

"It's right there by that drain," I said.

Elliot effortlessly glided to the bottom of the pool where the main suction drain was tilted open, gurgling as it skimmed the chlorine in a seesaw motion. He swam back up to the surface to catch his breath. "I think I see it," he said.

Elliot was not bright enough to know that I hadn't worn earrings since high school. He hadn't gifted me silver earrings for Christmas, nor had I worn any jewelry to the swimming pool that morning. By the time Elliot swum back to the bottom, I felt a darkness crowd my vision as the pool water reverberated so violently it was like a proper riptide in an ocean. The jets flipped on, steering the water into a riptide so he could not swim north. He tried outswimming the mystical and sudden tide as the water pumped viciously from all sides. The current picked up as manchineel leaves submerged from the drain and shrouded him like jellyfish.

Saint Grit pulsed through me, the wickedly curved talons of her deformed arms turning like a wheel, therefore turning the vacuum port into high-gear as the access hatch flipped off its axis and Elliot's body thrusted downward. His cock and the stiff jelly of his balls were grabbed by the rotating cuff inside the drain hatch. Blood spooled up to the surface. I ran, calling for an ambulance.

The girls and I sat in the family waiting unit outside of surgery and recovery listening to the tinging of phones and elevator doors as orderlies hauled laundry by. Everything smelled of rubbing alcohol and vinyl. Elliot's accident was caused by suction entrapment—that's what the paperwork said. A tragedy for him. It reminded me of Hatch's sink disposal misfortune.

Men could be so careless.

Elliot underwent a nine-hour penile amputation surgery. His urethra was severed by the circulating suction, nearly lacerating his large intestine by a quarter of an inch. He'd needed four blood transfusions. A microsurgeon had reconnected his arterial veins. He'd piss through a catheter for months.

When visitor's hours were over, I convinced the night nurse to let me stay a little longer. Elliot was pale, the blue trajectory of his veins bulging under sticky-tape that held in his numerous IVs pumping him of morphine and antibiotics. He'd lost a third of his blood volume. The urologist and plastic surgeon were unsure of his recovery time.

When Elliot awoke, he was angry with me and the night nurse noticed as she scribbled his vitals on paper. The rims of his eyes welled with tears. "You did this," he said, above a whisper. "You won't get away with this. You're the devil's creature."

Only an inch of Elliot's penis had been sown into an extra perineal sack below his pelvic bone, with a plastic bag hanging off his hip, draining him of blood. Flaccid as the town.

CHAPTER 14.

WHEN BECKETT WAS born he came out of me with his limbs encrusted in moss and gnarled cysts that deformed his neck. He was covered in broken feathers and had small, sharp teeth protruding out of his jaw. He was born feral, an afterbirth materialized into a freak. There was a small valley in my womb where he'd grown into one of the bony animal skull totems from previous years; the one in the sugarcane field, the one in the marsh. This one, I grew myself.

I'd had to remove Beckett with Pippa's help, digging around my entrails and organs. However, I was not afraid. I was not in agony either. I made Pippa dig into me for Beckett. "He's there," I told her, my head in the dirt on the edge of the triangle in the woods. "Come on, faster. Tug at that. Pretend it's rope." Junia wore a headlamp, casting white light over us so we could see.

"I am, Nadine," Junia said.

This was my woods, after all, my primitive ground. It was the summer of 1997 and it was time for my girls to bring Beckett to the old witch. Sugar Bends' townies would wonder why sap-black sludge oozed off the trees and the black smoke didn't rise.

Pippa had gone feral, too, that summer. She was embarrassed but couldn't help herself. I could see her fearfulness when she caught herself dropping to all fours and running like a stray dog that sees a rooster. She looked criminally insane. She'd bring a hand to her mouth and cry until she fell asleep, or stride up to her bedroom and slam the door. Once, she tried chewing her hand off. She begged for me to make her quit. "Can you make a spell; make it all go away."

On our final night of July 1997, Pippa heard the witch's horn for the first time. She got Junia out of bed and the three of us donned our red robes and went to unbury Beckett at the edge of the triangle. He was very alive, not fully buried so he didn't have a full supply of oxygen, but unable to squirm under the deadweight of leaves and twisted branches. He was rained on. He looked like a wet sea urchin. The girls missed him in between visits under the full moon. They worried about their brother, as if he was going to get up and leave. Beckett got all the nourishment he needed from the soil; no reason to eat or sleep. If he was sentient, which I suspected he was, it was only enough to cry, fuss, piss.

I despised Beckett, this third totem boy, this strange creature. He was hideous. I didn't know he would look like that upon being born. I wanted to get rid of him, finally. I'd had to wait until Pippa could hear the horn and in the same month that she turned thirteen, it happened. I didn't want to look at his ugly, rotting face anymore, scuffed with boils.

We wrapped him in a blanket, the stink sweat of wet pine in the air as we walked the long way to the water tower. The girls had never been there before. "It was where I met your father," I said. We marched down Flat Roads East and through Tidioute out to Mowry Road. I couldn't remember the night being this dark before, and although it was a half-moon shining brightly, the streetlights didn't do much to help guide our path.

"The horn's hurting my ears," Pippa whined. She caressed Beckett's branch-jetted skull. She blew him a kiss. "Can Beckett hear the horn?"

"I think he can," I said, smiling down at this monstrosity.

"I can't hear the horn," Junia said. "I think I'm still too young."

I'd told the girls recently that their father had left them for the Arizona desert. "Sedona," I said, like they had any idea. "Just like your grandfather left me. That's how men are." But that night, under the clear, gray sky, they saw Elliot decomposing in the underbrush by the red barn across from the water tower.

The girls did not accept this and screamed, crying obscenities of confusion, awakening the other half-alive men in the crabgrass. The old witch heard and moved like a shadow out of the barn. The refracted glow from the single lightbulb practically blotted out the rim of visible trees. She moved toward us like a snake emerging from a rock, throwing heat to the shivering grass. Everything ripened in the dark, even us.

We moved toward her carrying the totems in our arms, each of us bearing the gifts. The three totems. Beckett's eyes bulged in fright as he tried twisting free, having never used his legs or hips before. Pippa took off in a scramble of terror, dropping the totem, headed for the open field, but the witch grabbed her and took her into the barn. Junia ran after her sister and I joined six feet behind, listening to Saint Grit's bones snap all around, echoing through the trees like a gasp for breath. We went into the barn with the old witch where it was time for the ceremony, and Pippa begged to leave.

"Hail, Saint Grit!"

"Hail, Saint Grit!"

"Please, mama, Nadine—*no*!"

"Hail, Saint Grit!"

The shapes of my girls' bodies fringed with mold and the ground ruptured as the sound of the ancient ox horn played. The old witch gave me the hollow shell. Pippa begged, at first, to leave, but it was a slow burn. She intrinsically knew her place in the barn in the hottest center of Sugar Bends, Florida.

CHAPTER 15.

I AWOKE BACK at the house—vertical in a second story wall—enclosed in deafening silence. The house was not the same. All of the furniture had been moved out long ago except for a ratty beanbag chair in the corner. There's black mold on the ceiling, spread out over four splotches. Rain damage or decomposition, I do not know.

Voices echoed from downstairs. The girls? It couldn't be, the girls were taken by the witch. And it definitely wasn't Elliot. The strangers' voices floated upstairs and back down again before a door slammed shut—the old porch door with the broken hinge on the bottom. The door was unchanged.

I lifted my head off my shoulder and drifted to the second story window. It was daytime, the sky a shade of bruised crimson. The manchineels had been chopped down. Only their hairy roots and stumps remained. There's a For Sale sign where the *Welcome to Hatch Landing* sign used to stick out of the ground by the mailbox. I thought of the things I've buried in that yard; my self-induced orgasms and animal bones.

A giddy surge of joy washed over me when I thought of all the people I'd ever known in my life. Most of them were sacrificed to Saint Grit, in one decade or another, just enough for her to keep playing the ox horn. I could still hear it as clear as a cannon.

A moving truck rumbled up Suwanee Road. Somebody, a family, maybe, was moving into the old farm house. My house where I still occupied the rooms and the curved, moth-lived eaves, the drawers, the crawl spaces. I listened to the new owners traipse around the property, making noise, clutter. I wondered if they'd ever find their way out of a dark forest before without a map. I doted on the tree inside of me that would never burn.

ACKNOWLEDGEMENTS

Many thanks to Max Booth III and Lori Michelle for believing in this weird little book. Your commitment and enthusiasm for the spooky book community makes this genre a hundred times better because of it. I'm proud to be a ghoul. Many thanks to Alejandra Oviedo for the sexy, badass, nightmarish book cover. Many thanks to Betty Rocksteady for the amazing illustrations. Many thanks to Joey R. Poole and Beth Gilstrap for being Saint Grit's first readers—your feedback and time helped me improve not only my writing but the story, in all its many drafts. Many thanks to Nina for the homemade baked goods. Many thanks to my friend Annette for making a shitty day job better. Many thanks to Lev for distracting me with hours upon hours of video games. Many thanks to my cats Buster, Frankie, Ash, and the late Trinity for keeping me company while I'm writing.

Many thanks to my late granny, my QuQu, my first reader. Our imaginary mansion and you are forever in my heart.

Many thanks to C. R. Foster, my forever family, my booski, my creative compass. You've made me a better reader and writer. You inspire me. Thank you for your time, readership, laughter, and encouragement in all of Saint Grit's various stages and drafts. You bring the sun to the Pacific Northwest. I love you.

Many thanks to my husband, Serdar, whose endless love and support lifts me every day. You really are the Bob Belcher to my Linda Belcher. Thank you for giving me the time to write, making me laugh, keeping me fed, and loving me exactly as I am. You've never quit believing in my writing. Thank you for making life fun. I love you.

Profound thank you to anybody that reads this book.

ABOUT THE AUTHOR

Kayli Scholz is a writer from Florida. Her work has been published by Neon Hemlock Press, Ghoulish Books, Storychord, and others. She's currently working on other horror novels. She loves all things horror, cryptids, and her cats. She's online at kayli-scholz.com.

SPOOKY TALES FROM GHOULISH BOOKS 2023

LIKE REAL | Shelly Lyons
ISBN: 978-1-943720-82-8 $16.95
This mind-bending body horror rom-com is a rollicking Cronenbergian gene splice of *Idle Hands* and *How to Lose a Guy in 10 Days*. It's freaky. It's fun. It's LIKE REAL.

XCRMNTMNTN | Andrew Hilbert
ISBN: 978-1-943720-81-1 $14.95
When a pile of shit from space lands near a renowned filmmaker's set, inspiration strikes. Take a journey up a cosmic mountain of excrement with the director and his film crew as they ascend into madness led only by their own vanity and obsession. This is a nightmare about creation. This is a dream about poop. This is a call to arms against vowels. This is *XCRMNTMNTN*.

BOUND IN FLESH | edited by Lor Gislason
ISBN: 978-1-943720-83-5 $16.95
Bound in Flesh: An Anthology of Trans Body Horror brings together 13 trans and non-binary writers, using horror to both explore the darkest depths of the genre and the boundaries of flesh. A disgusting good time for all! Featuring stories by Hailey Piper, Joe Koch, Bitter Karella, and others.

CONJURING THE WITCH | Jessica Leonard
ISBN: 978-1-943720-84-2 $16.95
Conjuring the Witch is a dark, haunted story about what those in power are willing to do to stay in power, and the sins we convince ourselves are forgivable.

WHAT HAPPENED WAS IMPOSSIBLE |
E. F. Schraeder
ISBN: 978-1-943720-85-9 $14.95
Everyone knows the woman who escapes a massacre is a final girl, but who is the final boy? *What Happened Was Impossible* follows the life of Ida Wright, a man who knows how to capitalize on his childhood tragedies . . . even when he caused them.

THE ONLY SAFE PLACE LEFT IS THE DARK|
Warren Wagner
ISBN: 978-1-943720-86-6 $14.95

In *The Only Safe Place Left is the Dark*, an HIV positive gay man must leave the relative safety of his cabin in the woods to brave the zombie apocalypse and find the medication he needs to stay alive.

THE SCREAMING CHILD| Scott Adlerberg
ISBN: 978-1-943720-87-3 $16.95

Scott Adlerberg's *The Screaming Child* is a mystery horror novel told by a grieving woman working on a book about an explorer who was murdered in a remote wilderness region, only to get caught up in a dangerous journey after hearing the distant screams from her own vanished child somewhere in the woods.

RAINBOW FILTH | Tim Meyer
ISBN: 978-1-943720-88-0 $14.95

Rainbow Filth is a weirdo horror novella about a small cult that believes a rare psychedelic substance can physically transport them to another universe.

LET THE WOODS KEEP OUR BODIES| E. M. Roy
ISBN: 978-1-943720-89-7 $16.95

The familiar becomes strange the longer you look at it. Leo Bates navigates a broken sense of reality, shattered memories, and a distrust of herself in order to find her girlfriend Tate and restore balance to their hometown of Eston—if such a thing ever existed to begin with.

SAINT GRIT| Kayli Scholz
ISBN: 978-1-943720-90-3 $14.95

One brooding summer, Nadine Boone pricks herself on a poisonous manchineel tree in the Florida backcountry. Upon self-orgasm, Nadine conjures a witch that she calls Saint Grit. Pitched as *Gummo* meets *The Craft*, Saint Grit grows inside of Nadine over three decades, wreaking repulsive havoc on a suspicious cast of characters in a small town known as Sugar Bends. Comes in Censored or Uncensored cover.

Ghoulish Books
PO Box 1104
Cibolo, TX 78108

☐ LIKE REAL   16.95
☐ XCRMNTMNTN   14.95
☐ BOUND IN FLESH   16.95
☐ CONJURING THE WITCH   16.95
☐ WHAT HAPPENED WAS IMPOSSIBLE   14.95
☐ THE ONLY SAFE PLACE LEFT IS THE DARK   14.95
☐ THE SCREAMING CHILD   16.95
☐ RAINBOW FILTH   14.95
☐ LET THE WOODS KEEP OUR BODIES   16.95
☐ SAINT GRIT   14.95
    Censored | Uncensored

Ship to:

Name _____

Address _____

City_____State_____Zip _____

Phone Number _____

                          Book Total: $_____

                     Shipping Total: $_____

                       Grand Total: $_____

Not all titles available for immediate shipping. All credit card
purchases must be made online at GhoulishBooks.com. Shipping is
5.80 for one book and an additional dollar for each additional book.
Contact us for international shipping prices. All checks and money
orders should be made payable to Perpetual Motion Machine.

Patreon:
www.patreon.com/ghoulishbooks

Website:
www.Ghoulish.rip

Facebook:
www.facebook.com/GhoulishBooks

Twitter:
@GhoulishBooks

Instagram:
@GhoulishBookstore

Linktree:
linktr.ee/ghoulishbooks